THICKER THAN WATER

THICKER THAN WATER

COMING-OF-AGE STORIES BY
IRISH AND IRISH AMERICAN
WRITERS

Edited by Gordon Snell

DELACORTE PRESS

Y
5011795

Published by
Delacorte Press
an imprint of
Random House Children's Books
a division of Random House, Inc.
1540 Broadway
New York, New York 10036

Visit us on the Web! www.randomhouse.com/teens
Educators and librarians, for a variety of teaching tools, visit us at
www.randomhouse.com/teachers

Cataloging-in-Publication Data
Cataloging-in-Publication Data is available from the Library of Congress.
ISBN: 0-385-32571-1

The text of this book is set in 13-point Garamond #3.
Book design by Trish P. Watts
Manufactured in the United States of America
February 2001
10 9 8 7 6 5 4 3 2 1
BVG

To Maeve, and all my other great friends in Ireland

CONTENTS

INTRODUCTION

This remarkable collection was inspired by the fact that Ireland is a young country: around half of its population is under the age of twenty-five. For them, coming of age is a very recent or a present reality. Ireland, too, is coming of age, for within the lifetime of these young people the country has changed more dramatically than in any previous generation.

Today the Irish grow up in an exhilarating place full of new opportunities and ideas, where there is money to spend and jobs in plenty. Twenty or so years ago, the economy was struggling and jobs were scarce, so that many thousands had to emigrate to get work. Often they went to the United States, to Britain, or to Australia, and most of them flourished.

That tradition of emigration, by necessity or choice, goes back more than 150 years to the period of the Great

Famine (1845 to 1849), when thousands upon thousands of Irish people left the poverty and hunger of their homeland. They found a particular welcome in the United States, where many of them eventually rose to positions of power and importance. The Irish have always been a vivid presence in American life, and Ireland and America have always had a special connection.

The vitality of the youth culture of Ireland draws young people from all over the world, particularly to the sparkle and energy of cities like Dublin, the capital, and Galway on the west coast. Festivals up and down the country attract young musicians who play everything from traditional Irish music to rock. The Irish arts scene has had spectacular international success, with shows like *Riverdance,* the films of Neil Jordan, stars like Pierce Brosnan and Gabriel Byrne, and bands like Bono's U-2 and the Corrs—and Irish writers on the international scene are too numerous to mention.

Ireland now has a talented workforce for the information age whose skills have prompted many high-tech companies to set up there, helping to bring in the booming prosperity we call the Celtic Tiger.

What has not changed is the value the Irish people have always placed on storytelling. Ever since the ancient days when storytellers and poets moved around the country from town to town and village to village, the art of telling tales has been prized and revered. Even in ordinary conversation in Ireland, there are usually more talkers than listeners, and a newcomer can find it hard to get a word in edgeways.

Also unchanged, in Ireland as in other places, are the dreams, hopes, and anxieties of young people growing up, and the belief of each generation that no one before has ever experienced them so intensely.

These stories illustrate the great variety of the powerful feelings that surge through people who are coming of age—sometimes so powerful that they can seem ecstatic, or frightening and overwhelming.

Here are stories that explore the intense loyalty and hostility that exist side by side within communities, and within families. Other stories turn to the past, or highlight the generation gap between parents and children and the realization that parents are not the powerful or protecting figures they might once have seemed but are real people, flawed, loving.

Here you will find stories about passion and first love and physical discovery; and about self-hatred, and the feeling that everyone else is full of confidence and has got life sorted out. Learning that others feel just the same way as you do is one of the most liberating realizations of growing up. Here also are stories of triumph, of the freedom of a pioneering spirit, and of the discovery of strength and courage people never imagined they had.

It is exciting to live in a young country like Ireland, and

it has been a special delight to me to gather the stories of these writers from many different backgrounds and age groups, and to read about their own individual visions of growing up.

I hope you will enjoy them too, and enter into the Irish perspective on the universal experience of coming of age.

Gordon Snell

THICKER THAN WATER

WATERY LANES

by Shane Connaughton

All I ever wanted to do was see the stars in day-light. And there should be a law against charging a sixteen-year-old boy with murder. You reach that age and the testosterone starts blowing your lid off. Your brain can't cope until you're eighteen. But by then it's often too late. If there's a girl involved. In my case there was a girl involved.

We lived on the edge of town. There was a village surrounded by fields. Miles from the city. Then houses were built, roads put in, and overnight we were a sub-urb. They built a new runway at the airport and now we were under a flight path. My mother went crack-ers. My dad went to the pub.

My mother had rows with the neighbors. Mrs. Kelly got new shoes. She wore them round to our front gate and showed them to Mum.

"Haven't you got big feet?" my mother said.

Apparently this is an insult. Soon Mrs. Kelly was sobbing and shouting and other women had to tell my mother to go indoors "And stay there."

Mrs. Reilly got new wallpaper. When she invited Mum in for tea my mother told her with such wallpaper she might as well go all the way and open an Indian restaurant.

Now she and Mrs. Reilly didn't talk anymore. And the list was growing.

My father and his friends put it down to the overflying airplanes. "It's the noise. It can't be good for you. Them BAC One Elevens can crack stones goin' over, never mind heads."

My father put in double windows but it made little difference.

My mother took to needlework. Her meticulous fingers threaded the night to the morning. Then she died.

When her coffin was lowered into the grave a jumbo jet thundered above. Its shadow slowly ghosted across us, darkening the headstones all the way over to the cemetery wall. Wings but no angel.

I looked down into the hole. It was deep but the earthy floor was bright as noon.

I was fifteen years seven months that day.

I lived with my father now. Left for school in the morning, came home in the evening. Ate, studied, watched telly, looked at myself in the mirror, was pleased with what I saw, went to bed. I was five feet seven inches.

The house we lived in was a new redbrick one in a street that had ninety-eight others all the same. The only thing I liked about it was from an upstairs window you could see our old house in the Watery Lanes.

My father was born in that house and so was I. It was built with uncut stones and thick mortar and had an asbestos roof. It was down off the road right on the edge of a river. The river was six feet below the house and usually ran very narrow and shallow. We crossed it on a few wooden planks nailed together and this took us up to a wide green stretch of open ground where people walked dogs, kids played football, bigger lads grazed horses. Some kids dug a hole one day and a horse fell into it and had to be hauled out by the fire brigade. They put a sling under his belly and raised him up with a crane. For a moment he was up in the air, his legs dangling. His mane had fallen over his eyes so you couldn't see life. He looked like a big dead pantomime horse. But he was okay and when they lowered him and released him he gave a buck and ran off across the grass and out onto the road amongst the traffic.

Sometimes the river in winter rose high enough to flood into our house. It didn't come in the door or windows. It came up under the floors. That was why our beds had twelve-inch blocks of wood fixed to each leg. The water, in my history anyway, never reached the mattresses. The twelve-inch blocks were exact to a meteorological degree. We often went toward our beds in Wellingtons but on reaching them slept high and dry.

My granny lived with us. She had an expression for when things went wrong or weren't working out right. "It's all up in the air or down in the ground," she'd say.

When we were told we had to get out of the Watery Lanes, Granny took it bad. The man from the council said the house was going to be knocked, the river piped, covered in and built over. We were "an anachronism," he said.

Granny took this as a personal wounding.

"Knackers?" she shouted at him. "Get out of my house, you cheeky brat, before I ossify you."

I got the dictionary and explained the word to her and she went calm again. She had to accept the facts. Where we stood and sat at that moment would in a year be the dead center of a roundabout on the new motorway carrying traffic to the North and to the airport.

We had to move to one of the new houses no later than the first of the following February.

Granny died on Christmas day. She got out of bed and sat in her chair by the old black range. Mum and Dad were out at morning mass. I was sitting at the table playing my new harmonica. When I looked at Granny she was dead. She hadn't been eating enough. At her age, I expect you have to have willpower to eat.

The house filled with neighbors. They wouldn't move Granny until the doctor arrived. People drank tea and bottles of Guinness. And in the middle of them all Granny, in her nightdress, sat dead in her chair. It was a strange sight. Her long gray hair hung round her shoulders. She'd not got round to putting it up in its usual style. Her hair was her pride. Now it hung limp and reminded me of the mane of the poor horse rescued by the fire brigade. As people came in and out the door the drafty air stuck in her hair, shifting it a little. It was weird. Her ankles were thin as pins.

Granny was the end of the Watery Lanes. The old people cried a lot at her funeral. Her end was the writing on the wall for them too.

It's amazing how quick a house falls down. The cold winds and vandals can tear it apart in a few months. Someone even stole the asbestos roof. I'd skip over from our new house and walk through the dereliction. I'd lean out the shattered kitchen window and look down on the river. When Granny made tea she'd shake the old tea leaves from the pot out the window and into the water. Except they never reached the water. They'd fall onto the muddy bank and over the year accrue into a brown mound. She liked her tea strong and plentiful. Before the winter flood rose that mound was bigger than a garden tub.

I was hanging out the window one evening looking down on the tea-stained mud when I was joined by a kid I knew. He had a spade and shovel and told me he was on his way to dig a hole with some friends. The bulldozers and earthmoving machinery were eating up the park but there were lots of places left in the middle of the chaos for holes. If you dug a hole deep enough, he said, you could see the stars in daylight. The stars were there in the sky all the time. Not just at night. But if you went deep into the earth and looked up, even at noon, you'd see them.

This was for kids. Now I was sixteen so I forgot about it. I was also six feet tall and skinny. One night I went to bed five feet seven and next morning when I got up I was six feet. This is gospel. I couldn't get into my trousers. Well, I could, but they finished just below my kneecaps. I had to borrow a pair of my father's to go to school. It was so embarrassing. And on the way home I met a girl at the bus stop. She looked at me and didn't laugh. She was wearing a school uniform and was bursting out of it in all the best places. Next day same bus stop, different trousers, I asked her out.

"Where to?"

"I'll show you the Watery Lanes."

In the old house she told me I'd better not touch her in any of her best places or her uncle would murder me.

Her uncle was Horace McDermott the famous computer artist. He did paintings and drawings on a computer and got a lot of money for them from rich folk who went to art galleries. Most of these works of art depicted his niece. My girlfriend. And I loved her. And her name was and still is Dee McDermott.

I called for her one evening to her house. Horace McDermott turned out to be a big sack of spuds with a massive beard. It came down to his belly and apparently got caught a lot in car doors and sink plug holes. He wore a black hat which I suppose he thought gave him a distinctive artistic air. It did. Distinctive as in ridiculous. I couldn't keep a straight face. So he chased me. He chased me many times. He was jealous. Dee was his niece and model and no young fellah like me was getting anywhere near her.

He was wrong about this. One night Dee met me in the Watery Lanes. She was wearing a white summer dress and her hair was tied back so I could see her neck. I kissed her on the back of the neck first and she said she liked that. Then I nibbled her ears and she liked that even better.

Soon I was the best lover in our street of ninety-eight houses. And every time Horace McDermott saw me coming he made a tear after me and I had to take rapidly to my very long legs. I now knew why nature had given them to me. His black hat, with its very wide rim, always blew off when he chased me and he always went back to retrieve it. So it was no contest. Why did he wear such a hat? And beard? And why did he wear dark glasses even on a sunless day? Fashion is a strange disease. You wear dark glasses so you can see people but the people can't see you. They can't see into your eyes. So people who wear dark glasses on sunless days must be guilty about something. Pop stars wear them all the time. It's obvious what they're guilty about. Their music.

I began to teach Dee about music. I'd play my

harmonica for her. She liked the Otis Rush classic "My Love Will Never Die." She'd lie back looking at me with her big brown mushroom eyes, her legs crossed and one foot in the air tapping in time. I'd stop often and kiss her foot and soon my lips would be soft as butterfly wings on her thighs. This she liked. She let me kiss along the inside of her thighs. That's something.

I told her one day about seeing the stars in daylight. I said I'd dig a really deep hole and put straw in the bottom and we could lie on it, make love and look up at the stars.

"Yeah? Cool," she said.

The bulldozers and machinery were all round now and our street and streets a long way away were covered in gray, dirty dust. When it rained it was worse. The cars were filthy, the streets running muddy grime.

My father complained a lot but he paid me to wash the Fiat. He also warned me against Horace McDermott.

"He's one bollocks, that fellah. It was his family sure, sold all the land to the council. His family owned the Watery Lanes. Did you not know that? He's an artist all right. A bleedin' con artist. He's got political connections, that fellah."

Dee and I went to a gallery off Grafton Street to see

his work. One piece was called *Dee Baby*. It was supposed to be her but all it was was straight lines and geometric graphics. It lacked sensuosity.

"Is there such a word?" she asked.

"Yes. You are it. In that dead printout where are your best places?"

"I see what you mean. He had his hand on my tummy when he was doing that one."

I was furious. I was going to confront McDermott. Incidentally the gallery was asking seven thousand punts for *Dee Baby*.

I went up the garden path of his big house and rang the bell. It chimed out a piece of Ravel's *Bolero*. I almost puked. He came to the door. He had a big white napkin in his hand and was wiping down his beard. There was half a slice of bread hanging out of it. What made that man think he was an artist? Beard plus hat plus dark glasses plus computer equals Toulouse-Lautrec.

"McDermott—you're a fraud. If you had any talent you'd shave off that chin weed. You'd also come out from behind those sunglasses. What are you—a secret policeman? And keep your podgy hands off Dee's tummy at all times. Flesh into a computer does not go. I am a man in love. Understand?"

He knocked the wind out of my sails by appearing

very calm. He stayed silent for a minute whilst he dealt with the batch loaf in his beard. He stood there looking at the bread and mangling it to crumbs between his fingers. Then he dropped the crumbs to the ground and flicked his fingers along his thumbs like a priest during mass shaking off any remnants of clinging Host.

"What are your intentions with my only niece? Give me a cogent reply and I'm prepared to desist from calling the police."

"I'm digging a hole near the Watery Lanes and we're going to go down into it and whilst making love, see the stars in daylight."

"You're a complete headbanger, chum."

He jumped at me and caught me by the front of my new shirt. I caught him by the only thing I could— his beard. It felt like hanks of horsehair. We struggled around the garden, muttering and groaning and then because it was stalemate we let each other go. He was panting really badly. At that moment I felt sorry for him and peculiarly chastened. He was only a sack of spuds with a beard and hat and dark glasses and I was a six-foot broom handle. I knew, having felt him, he was a fraud. How is it that fraudsters are always rich? They are in the art world anyway. I knew about the art world because on account of Horace McDermott I started reading *The Irish Times*. They always had stuff about painters, most of whom seemed to be Horace McDermott.

By now school was out the window. You can't do exams and have a rampant sex life at the same time. I'd only go to school because of the bus stop. And meeting Dee there. And great words I'd find in the school dictionary. For example—*pulchritudinous.*

"To me, Dee, you are pulchritudinously perfect. A beauty rare enough to cause a traffic pileup."

"Why bring traffic into it?"

"All your best places are pneumatically perfect. If you were a bicycle . . ." This was a metaphor with instantly apparent double entendre. I quickly punctured it.

"Why bring bicycles into it? I don't own one."

"No, what I mean is, the erectile eagerness of your embosomed charms knocks miracles for six."

"For six what?"

"I'm talking about your nipples, Dee."

"Well, don't—there's a bus coming."

She was down-to-earth all right. Beside her the word *prosaic* was skittish and exciting. She was so sure of her beauty she didn't have to have words confirming the fact. I never questioned my luck. Here I was and she was here beside me. At her school she was doing physics, geography, and chemistry. So she was intrigued by my hole-in-the-ground idea.

I dug in a spot near the river. During the day yellow earthmoving machinery the size of a herd of dinosaurs raped what was left of the landscape. But in the evenings the place belonged to me and a hundred other dreamers. I dug into the earth. Brown clay first, then black, then gray and stony. Kids helped me. When I got down to six feet and could no longer throw up the soil we had a bucket on a rope which I filled and the kids dragged up and emptied. We made long ladders from scraps of wood so we could easily get up and down ourselves. When my father heard about the hole he told me I was too big now for such childish adventure. I didn't tell him about the straw and Dee's heavenly body at the bottom of my dream.

It was hard work digging. And sometimes the sides of the pit gave way and fell in. This was scary. I had to hammer in some shuttering to keep the sides apart. By the time I'd dug down twelve feet I'd reached limestone bedrock. I could go no further.

I was tired. The bulldozers were getting closer to the spot as well. I couldn't see the stars in daylight when I looked up. But I told the kids I could. And they came down the ladders and lay on the floor and peered up into the grave-sized sky and swore blind they saw stars. "Yeah, there they are. Bleedin' magic."

I told Dee my planetarium was ready. The fellah who owned the horse gave me the straw. We chose the day of the All Ireland Football Final for our descent into heaven. The Watery Lanes teemed with people but on that day everyone would be inside watching the match on telly. Dublin were in the final and a fellah round our way was playing for them. I saw him shifting his big thick neck to look at Dee as we walked through the shopping center one Saturday. So I was praying they were going to get beaten. At any rate dogs, cats, humans would all be glued to the box.

We lay in each other's arms and saw the stars everywhere but in the sky. But it didn't matter. We would have had to dig much deeper for it to have worked. But I could never have dug deeper than my love for Dee. And she told me that afternoon that she loved me. We held hands going home and stood in the middle of the wasteland of concrete, clay, steel, culverts, approaching motorway and flyover, and whispered the three words—*I love you*. I said them. She said them. And I never break my word.

Someone had seen us emerging from the hole and told Horace McDermott. That night he came after me. He had a claw hammer in his hand and I knew he wanted to fix my head with it. I ran and he trotted. But he kept on coming. I ran down into the Watery Lanes and hid in our old house. But I heard his heavy feet on the uneven ground and I made for the one place I knew he'd never find. The hole. Stargazers' paradise. But he saw me and kept on coming. He clambered up over mounds of earth and gravel left by the construction gangs and kept on in pursuit. Why? Why was he so angry? Dee no longer lived in his house and had returned to her parents. He blamed me for this. He was right. But apart from that . . .

I didn't go down into the hole because I realized if he managed to find me I'd be a sitting duck there. The last I saw of Horace he was at the hole on his knees and hammering at the shuttering with the claw hammer. Night was down and the sky was bright with stars strewn about like diamonds in the blue. His great shadow bulked through the dark—the beard, the wide-brimmed hat. He shouted after me, his chin raised to the sky—"I'll be dug out of you, chum. You've ruined our lives."

There was such feeling in his voice it troubled me. It made me think of my hatred for him. I decided not to hate him ever again. I walked across the blasted territory. A length of steel lay on the ground. It shone with starlight. It was a silvery stream of stars. The moon lay deep in a puddle. I was as lonely as that moon. I was as distant from it as Horace McDermott was from me. Water is strange. An old puddle on a vast construction site can bed the moon down for the night. The moon takes root in puddles. That's like love. Mine took root in the Watery Lanes.

At home my father was reading a circular from the council. It stated our area would no longer be called Finglas. From here to eternity we would be known as County Fingal. The difference was of bureaucratic proportions only. It would appear on tax demands and council bills but no native would use it in ordinary conversation. It would also appear on a big sign on the new motorway—WELCOME TO COUNTY FINGAL. TWINNED WITH CANTON, MASSACHUSETTS, USA. SPONSORED BY PREMIER DAIRIES.

"The whole place is up in the air," my father said, "or down in the ground."

Weeks went by before it was realized Horace McDermott was missing. The newspapers went ape. This was big stuff. Horace McDermott was Ireland's answer to the world's question. If art was an Olympic sport, with Horace we had at least three gold medals in the bag. Except that Horace was missing.

Here's what I think happened. He was mucking about at the hole, venting his rage, when the thing collapsed and he fell in. Or he fell in and knocked himself out. So on the Monday morning when the earthmoving machines set to work and leveled the site and filled in the hole Horace was buried underneath. Without anyone knowing. Two days later the Watery Lanes was a concrete stretch of motorway. A few weeks later the whole of the Watery Lanes was a vast roundabout. And all over the shopping center were posters offering a reward for any information as to the whereabouts of the artist Horace McDermott.

Dee and I went round to his house one night. There was no reply to Ravel's *Bolero*. The house was heavy, empty. Lonely. In the thick ivy growing up the front, blackbirds nested. Disturbed by us, they flew in and out of the ivy. Each time they did so it triggered the security light. We sat on the garden wall for ages. The light would come on with a sound like the click of furtive wings. Stay bright for a short time, then cut out.

Dee announced she was finishing with me. She told me in the dark. And when the light plinged on I could see she was serious.

"Is it because you suspect me of murder?"

"It is because I'm going out with Mike Flynn. The bus conductor."

That was the end of that. Mike Flynn. No contest.

He had money, I didn't. He had a bus as well, for God's sake.

Down either side of my nose ran watery lanes. I covered them with my sleeve.

Next morning the police nabbed me on the way out to school. I swore blind I hadn't touched Horace McDermott. Which I hadn't. I told them my theory—he was under the new roundabout. I swore on my mother's grave. I pleaded testosterone. The detective wouldn't allow that. On account of it making him join the force in the first place. I cried my love for Dee. That was disallowed as well. On account of the detective suffering the same affliction himself. The sergeant's wife in his case.

"This is a crime of the person," he explained to me. "You're in serious trouble, my old pox bottle."

"I'm telling you. Horace McDermott is looking up at wheels."

"We can't dig the roundabout up. The Minister for Transport is opening it in a few days. It's a big occasion. Sponsored by Premier Dairies, for God's sake."

He flicked through a file and paused at a newspaper clipping. He read it aloud.

"Horace McDermott, the Irish computer artist, was yesterday charged at Southwark Crown Court, London, with throwing an empty Guinness bottle onto the stage during a performance of *A Little Night Music* at the National Theatre. He told the judge it was a protest at the cheap bourgeois sentimentality of the show." He closed the file.

"That's the kind of great man Horace was," the detective said, "and you murdered him."

"I did not."

"Don't annoy me now. This is 1996. We got the most modern equipment for solving these cases. You're not getting away with it."

He charged me with murder but I knew he was only testing. I walked out free.

Well, free but unhappy. I saw the bus roar round the roundabout and sitting on the side seat near the door was Mike Flynn with his arm round the piece of heaven who showed me the stars. If I ever become an astronomer and find a previously undiscovered planet I shall christen it Dee. I shall find a field, if there are any such items left by then, lie on my back and gaze all night at those lovely legs and mushroom eyes.

I suppose I'll dream too of Finglas river in winter babbling under my bed. A lost river. Running only in dreams. Buried forever under tons of concrete. But dreams keep on bubbling to the surface. Water cannot be hemmed, penned, tanked, piped, hidden. I will carry it in my head. From time to time it will burst out and drown people.

I stood with my father a distance away and watched

the Minister for Transport and other such formally open the motorway and roundabout. The minister called it a red-letter day for County Fingal. The police had the traffic stopped. Then the minister cut a tape and the cars and juggernauts leaped forward right over the spot where we were born and where Horace Mc-Dermott I am sure lies dead. No one who saw me watching could hear the malicious beatings of my culverted heart.

County Fingal last week stuck a sign up saying the roundabout was now called Horace McDermott Way.

I'll soon be eighteen. I'll soon be nineteen. But love never dies.

SHANE CONNAUGHTON

SHANE CONNAUGHTON lives in Finglas, Dublin, with his wife, Ann; his mother-in-law, Marie; his dog, Kilty, and his cat, Hector the Queer Viking. His daughter, Tara, is in New York; his son, Tom, in London. Shane Connaughton won the Hennessy Award for New Irish Writing in 1985, and in 1989 his first novel, *A Border Station,* was short-listed for the GPA Award. In 1990 he was an Academy Award nominee for the screenplay of *My Left Foot.* His second novel, *The Run of the Country,* was filmed in 1994. His book on the making of this film, *A Border Diary,* was published in 1995.

DOT ON THE i

by Jenny Roche

Bernadette Roe. Bernadette Anne Roe. Bernadette Anne Judith Roe. Bernie wrote her name on the inside back page of her Irish folder. Long columns of different styles and combinations. Up at the blackboard Miss Hughes wrote long columns of her own— the rules of the future conditional tense. Bernadette Anne Judith Roe. Judith was a recent addition. Since her confirmation last year.

"Judith?" her mother said. "God, in our day they made you take a saint's name." Judith was in the Bible. Bernie saw her as slightly dark-skinned and Jewish with some kind of colored scarf wrapped around her head. Or Judith Krantz who wrote the books she sneaked from beside her mother's bed.

Up at the board a film of chalk dust hung on Miss

Hughes's ancient brown cardigan, the one she'd definitely be found dead in as she never took it off. Every time she cleared a space with the duster a cloud of chalky white burst in the air and the specks spun for a second in the thin beam of sunlight that strayed briefly through the window from the street outside. Bernadette, Bernie, Berni. Bernie had decided to be Berni when she went into secondary school. Berni Roe. She liked the way it ended with the dot on the *i*. It was carefree, even cheeky, and she'd written it on everything—her new books, her folders, notebooks, even her pencil case and her PE skirt. But the teachers called her Bernadette and her friends were still the same ones she'd had in primary school, so after six long months she was still just Bernie. Except for her mother. Her mother wrote "To *B-e-r-n-i*" on her birthday card last month but that wasn't what she wanted. It had embarrassed her and for some strange reason made her want to cry.

The brief stream of sunlight disappeared back out the window and the chalk dust seemed to settle on the back of Bernie's teeth. In the desk beside her Mary Downes ruled margins in her folders. One red, one green—perfect straight lines on every page, in every folder, Mary Downes had ruled enough margins to last her the whole five years of secondary school and beyond. Perfect red and green margins until the end of time.

The clock behind Miss Hughes still stood at five minutes past three, the same as when Bernie last looked at it nine hours ago. Maybe it was stopped . . . what a present that would be, if it were really twenty minutes later than she thought, or better still nine hours, and she were actually fast asleep in bed oblivious to her life. But the minute hand jerked forward and quivered with silent laughter and then it stopped and stood still. At six minutes past three.

Bernie stared at her name on the page and all the Bernadettes and Bernies blurred and merged into stringy gray thoughts of the rest of the day. Fourteen minutes till the bell, the corridor, the noise of girls' voices, the toilets, the mirror, the next class. Business studies. Business studies was the next class. Business studies and then math. The two subjects she hated most, one after the other. Then home. Bit of television, dinner, then nothing. The whole evening and night, nothing. She couldn't even have a cookie now because of her diet. Then bed. Bernie thought about fainting, about slipping down languid as silk, down her seat, under the desk. Into two strong faceless arms and some light bright airy other place. She attached the business studies teacher's face to the arms. Mr.

Creighton, whose presence made her feel a little giddy when he stood beside her desk even though the pinkness under his skin gave him the look of a thin blond pig. But although the arms were warm and strong the airy place filled up with the red and green margins and rows and rows of figures that never balanced out.

"Look at her." Mary Downes's arm nudged hers. "She's at it again." At the top of the class Miss Hughes had gazed off in thought, and her hand slipped unconsciously beneath her chalky brown cardigan to fiddle with her bra. Bernie looked instead at Mary Downes's arm on the desk beside hers. Bare from the elbow beneath the rolled-up sleeve, slim, hairless, smooth, and a golden olive color. An antelope, Bernie thought at least ten times a day. An elegant antelope beside a hairy molly slug ape. She'd shaved her own arms last month with her father's razor, revealing smooth pink and white mottle, and now the hair had grown back, stubbly and dark.

Mary Downes elbowed her again. Miss Hughes's worn gray bra strap had made a doleful appearance. Giggles began to percolate and leak from the desks. Miss Hughes returned to her body with a flash of irritation and with a single sweep of the duster she wiped the future conditional from the board.

"Test tomorrow, girls," she said. "We'll see how smart you all are then."

Of all the years of Bernie's life this one was the longest and it was still only March. For the first time in her life she could think of nothing to look forward to. Every year she could remember (and she could remember back to age two) had been neatly divided into things to look forward to. Birthday, Saint Patrick's Day, Easter, summer holidays, Halloween, Christmas, and then start all over again. Always in the back of her head, even when she wasn't thinking about it, was the certainty of something good to come. And not just occasions . . . other things too . . . like the dog having pups, or getting ten pounds from her granddad, or shopping with her mother on a Saturday in town.

But this year was different and she didn't know why. It wasn't like the same things she'd always looked forward to weren't still there. They were but it was as if a silent steamroller had come and flattened them all into one long length of dough that just stretched on and on forever. And everything that happened just got rolled into the dough. Like going into secondary school, the biggest thing in her life, just got rolled on, and stretched out, one day after another, and she just sat, a fat blob in a classroom where she couldn't do the math.

Or moving to the new house with Bernie's own new room, which her mother told her she could paint herself—champagne and ivory or a mural by the bed. But then they moved and the new house seemed big and cold and empty and the old house and the little things Bernie'd known all her life and never noticed—the taps in the bathroom, the carpet on the stairs, the way the back door stuck—were suddenly unbearably precious and gone. She stuck up a couple of posters and left her room at that.

And her birthday. A teenager at last. They all made a fuss, especially her mother. But it was all the wrong shape. A teenager, her mother, her clothes, herself. She didn't know how it should be but this wasn't it. And her clothes were too tight. They were always too tight. There was nothing she could look forward to. Dinners made her fat, Christmas was just for kids, and in town on Saturdays now she walked two steps behind her mother so that anyone watching wouldn't think they were together.

When the bell went at four Bernie thought of her dinner. A quick rush of color and then she remembered. The diet. She'd have to say she wasn't hungry.

"Put it in the fridge for later then," her mother'd say, her mouth half full. Then all that would be left would be homework and bed.

In the toilets Bernie covered up the damp spot on

her underpants with a wad of folded-up toilet paper and secured it with her tights pulled way up around her waist. She felt dry and secure then but she knew it wouldn't last. Drip, drip, drip . . . her body oozing day and night now . . . secretions or whatever . . . she'd never get used to it . . . but she'd have to . . . it was normal . . . get used to walking around like this for the rest of her life.

She emerged from the stall and appeared in the mirror where Mary Downes stood waiting for her. Watching her face loom big and shiny and red behind Mary Downes's olive gold perfection. It's like a joke, Bernie thought. Beauty and the Beast. Beauty and the red shiny Beast. It would have made her laugh if she'd seen it somewhere else and the Beast wasn't her. She jerked her gaze away and washed every last germ from her hands under the tap.

"If you can't do the math," Mary Downes said in the cloakroom, "you can cog mine in the morning." She zipped up the front of her new red ski jacket.

"Thanks," said Bernie, zipping up her own. It was the same as Mary Downes's except that it was blue. At least she was better at English and art.

In the car park outside the school Mr. Creighton the business studies teacher slammed shut the door of his rusty blue car. In his rearview mirror Bernie thought she saw him smile at Mary Downes. She glanced quickly at Mary but her face showed no reaction. It had started to rain and the evening grew in dark over the town already. Even though it was March the days weren't getting any longer.

The two girls walked in close against the wall all down the Dublin road.

"My father's working late today," Mary Downes said when they got down to the square. "We'll have to get a lift home with John O'Reilly."

Normally they got a lift home with Mr. Downes when he finished work at five. They both lived in the same townland now, a few miles out of town, so it made perfect sense.

"Okay," Bernie said, and she pulled up the hood of her ski jacket over her face so the rain wouldn't clog up her glasses.

"Turn on your wipers," John O'Reilly had said the last time they'd driven home with him. It was the only thing he'd ever said directly to Bernie herself.

In McGuire's shop on Church Street Mary Downes bought two bags of Tayto salt-and-vinegar chips. She'd switched from smoky bacon not long ago and said there was absolutely no comparison. Through the window they could see John O'Reilly's car across the street in front of the Cash and Carry where he'd worked ever since he left school. Even through the rain they could see the pink furry dice suspended from the mirror and the cellophane strip in the back window proclaiming his taste in music. Inside the car the gear stick was a 3-D naked woman.

"You know," Mary Downes had said, swiveling around in the front seat the first time Bernie was in the car, "Lena thinks that's Our Lady."

Lena was John O'Reilly's mother. Bernie had laughed along with Mary and John O'Reilly but she had found it hard to and now she looked out the window every time he changed gears.

"Are you not getting anything?" Mary Downes opened up the second bag of Taytos.

"Naw," said Bernie. The smell of the Taytos made her stomach vicious with desire. Mary Downes munched noisily and the rain fell doggedly on huddled passersby. In the window display a faded beach ball sat left over from some summer past.

Bernie thought of her dinner. Curry most likely. And rice. Her mother put raisins in her curry and Bernie always picked them out. She could smell it and taste it almost and already she knew she'd end up eating it after all and then spend the whole night like every night swearing not to put so much as a cornflake into her mouth all the next day.

"You know Audrey Sweeney," Mary said.

Audrey Sweeney sat beside Mary Downes in German class when Bernie had music.

"Yes," said Bernie. Mary shook the crumbs of the Taytos into her palm and popped them in her mouth. She folded the package carefully and put it in her pocket. Later at home she'd shrink it under the grill and add it to her collection of melted miniature Tayto bags.

"You know her sister in fifth year?" Bernie thought for a minute. She couldn't place the girl but it didn't really matter. Mary's face was poised and sharp with information.

"Yeah, I think so," Bernie said.

"Well she's got bulimia, Audrey told me." Mary dusted the salt from her hands and swiped the residue on her uniform.

"That's terrible," said Bernie.

"I know," said Mary Downes. "It's disgusting. Audrey said her father had a fit when he found out. He said he wasn't working his arse off to put good food on the table for her to go and feed it to the toilet."

"And you know," said Mary Downes, "she's not even that thin."

When John O'Reilly levered the front seat forward for her to climb into the back, Bernie kept her head down so he wouldn't see her glasses. The rain had blown in sideways as they'd run across the road and speckled up the lenses but he didn't even look at her. A sad fat spotted owl, she thought, sitting in the back, and the heat in the car turned the speckles to fog so she couldn't even see. Invisible as well. A fogged-up invisible lump, she sank into the semidarkness and the smell of the car . . . boisterous synthetic pine from the air freshener that swung with the dice, her own wet coat, the also furry seat covers and John O'Reilly's hair. There was a dark spot on the ceiling directly above his head from the years of occasional contact. Bernie wondered if he knew. In the front seat Mary Downes chatted and laughed and flicked the pink dice with her finger. Bernie laughed too although only snippets of the chat drifted back to her through the sound of the rain and the car heater. She ducked and bent her head to one side whenever John O'Reilly looked in his rearview mirror so as not to impede his view. At night she'd remember all the witty, suggestive things she almost said.

Outside Bernie's house John O'Reilly's car skidded to a halt, scattering gravel from beneath the wheels hard against the gate. Instinctively Bernie glanced to the front window to see if anyone was watching. She knew her father considered John O'Reilly the worst kind of eejit, and if he saw her getting out of his car now he'd say it later and she'd feel compelled to say he wasn't. For some strange reason.

"Thanks a million." She said it casually and perky as John O'Reilly bent himself and the seat forward to let her out from behind. As she scrambled out onto the gravel she felt cold air against her legs, high, high up her legs it slapped hard against her buttocks, then it whipped around her stomach before freezing her heart dead with a terrible awareness.

There was a screech of laughter from the car and she stood immobile in the driveway, the skirt of her uniform bunched neatly and completely under the elastic of her ski jacket, her entire bum in the tights exposed woolly and hopeless in the wind and the rain in front of John O'Reilly's car.

She reached back in panic to pull it loose. It must have somehow ridden up in the low backseat of the car. But it was way too late.

"Here's me head, me arse is coming," John O'Reilly roared, laughing, and the furry dice danced. "And a fine arse it is."

The door slammed shut on the laughter and the car screeched away down the dark wet road.

Bernie's mother seemed tired as she spooned curry and rice onto plates for Bernie to carry to the table. The heat from the stove showed on her face.

"Are you all right?" she said. "You're very quiet."

"I'm fine," said Bernie, and turned quickly to the table, where the rest of the family sat waiting for their dinner. Alone of all the rooms in the new house Bernie liked the kitchen. The heat from the cooking made it seem warm and safe and the clatter of her brothers and sisters covered up her everlasting shame and stupidity.

"Here's me head, me arse is coming." Bernie really wasn't hungry now, but as if in time to their laughter and the car door slamming she ate fork after fork, raisins and all.

"Looks like you found your appetite," her mother said. "There's more but you better get it before someone else does."

Bernie saw again the eternity of her exposed bum in the wind, the gusset of her wool tights, the thick black seam down the middle and O God as well, the wad of toilet paper she still had in her underpants. The curry swelled now underneath those same tights and underpants, elastic upon elastic burning into her belly. If a belly could be throttled she'd be quite dead now. A fat, stupid disgrace and lump, she would be far better dead. A sudden clear thought stood up from the mess. Audrey Sweeney's sister. Bernie went and filled her plate again.

It was cold in the upstairs bathroom, the floor bare and the walls still only half tiled. Bernie locked the door and raised the toilet seat. It all seemed suddenly so simple. She stared at her fingers and they seemed to shake slightly. Nerves or just the cold? Then she stuck them down her throat. Nothing happened, then hey presto it worked. Worked brilliantly, brilliant. Brilliant, brilliant, brilliant. Again and again her fingers went down and again and again her stomach complied.

She stood up and flushed the toilet. She watched all that food magically disappear beneath a rush of fresh new water. Carefully she wiped any spatters away with toilet paper. She scrubbed her hands and teeth and even combed her hair.

Bernie opened the window and sprayed her mother's perfume into the air. Then she sat on the closed toilet seat and let the cool air from the window blow against her face. She felt tired and weak and pure. She thought of the evening ahead and how she wanted to go downstairs and be happy and lively with her family because they'd never in a million years suspect what she could do now. She thought of spring coming and then summer, and the high narrow walls that had grown up along her life in the past year seemed to crumble and fall. She felt giddy and light and at the same time, clear and firm.

She breathed in the sharp night air and with her finger traced her name on the window ledge. Over and over again. *B-e-r-n-i, B-e-r-n-i, B-e-r-n-i.* With a dot on the *i*.

JENNY ROCHE

JENNY ROCHE is from Tuam, County Galway. She works as a filmmaker, writer, actress, and mother and lives in Ireland. For many years she divided her time between Ireland and New York. She was a member of the New York Irish women's arts collective Banshee and a regular contributor of articles on the arts to *The Irish Voice*. Her short films and videos have appeared in international festivals; as an actress, she has appeared on Broadway, off-Broadway, and in independent films. Her story "Just Fine" was included in *The Hennessy Book of Irish Fiction*.

WHEN GRANIA GROWS UP

by Maeve Binchy

Grania was the youngest of the family. By a long way.

Her friend Lizzie was very interested in this.

"Maybe they tried and tried to have another child for ages after Sean, and then lo suddenly eight years later you arrived," Lizzie would say.

"Maybe." Grania wanted to change the subject.

She didn't like to think of her parents trying and trying to have another baby.

She didn't like to think about that sort of thing at all in connection with Mam and Dad. Nobody did, surely.

They seemed to be very fond of her; they were always saying that things would happen "when Grania grows up." Like they'd all go to America for a holiday or they'd let the house for the summer when Grania grows up.

Sometimes they sounded sad, like they wouldn't need so much room when Grania grows up, or there wouldn't be any music in the house.

Grania thought they must have been a bit lonely when Sean was about seven. And that they were delighted with her. She saw nothing odd about it at all.

But Lizzie shrugged. She did think it was strange to have such a gap in the family. In her own case it had all happened over a short period. There were three in the family, Lizzie, thirteen, her sister, twelve, and her next sister, eleven. And then no more truck with that sort of thing.

But Grania's family! Lizzie would say in wonder. Would you look at them, Patrick, twenty-three, Catherine, twenty-two, and Sean, twenty-one. Wasn't it a miracle they had tried again when they were so old and had Grania, otherwise she might not have existed at all.

"I could have been a butterfly instead," Grania said.

"Yeah, or a bulldog," Lizzie said.

Lizzie didn't know just how hurtful she could be, comparing Grania to a bulldog or a cart horse or an elephant! Lizzie was so small and delicate like a little elf herself. She never seemed to realize how awful it was not to be able to get clothes to fit you, and for people to say "Is this the little baby of the family? Heavens, hasn't she grown into a big girl?"

So Grania didn't sulk at her friend.

"Yeah, a bulldog or a lamb," she said good-naturedly.

"God, I'd hate to have been a lamb," Lizzie said. "People looking on you as a future dinner the moment you're born."

Grania's brother Patrick worked in a bar in New York. He sometimes sent her little gifts, like shiny hair ornaments once, or luminous Day-Glo pink socks or a belt which didn't fit her. Always he wrote a note saying that he would come home and see her sometime, but in the meantime she was never to forget her big brother in the Big Apple. And if ever she needed him she only had to call.

Grania wondered why she would *need* Patrick. It would be nice to see him; she wished he would come back.

Lizzie said there had been a coldness between Patrick and Grania's dad, some row a few years back. It was awful really that Lizzie knew so much about her family. Lizzie's mother talked a lot in front of the children. Grania's mam and dad didn't much.

Well, there was only Grania at home after all.

Catherine lived with her boyfriend, Gerry. They ran a market stall together, and lived in a mobile home. Catherine was very nice to Grania; she dropped in about once a week and gave her a small fresh tomato or a peach. "You don't want to be eating all those old sugary things, they only rot your teeth."

Grania knew it was because they made you fat but her sister never said anything like that.

Sometimes Catherine would jerk her head toward upstairs, in the direction of Mam and Dad's room.

"They're not getting you down, are they?" she would ask.

"No, why?"

"Ah, you know."

"No, they're great."

"Well, if ever they're not, you can always come to me and Gerry, you know that, don't you?"

"I do." Grania would nod solemnly, because Catherine sounded serious, but in her heart she had no idea why she would ever be driven to visit her sister and Gerry in that crowded caravan.

Her brother Sean worked in a record store. He used to tape copies of new releases for Grania, but he told her under pain of terrible punishment never to tell anyone he did it for her; she was to pretend she had done it herself from the radio; even though that was illegal too it wasn't as bad as what he was doing. Sean's friends had a couple of rooms nearer the center of town where his record shop was, so he often stayed with them, rather than coming home. But he brought his washing back home a couple of nights a week, and would sit in the kitchen talking to Grania as his clothes whirled about in the machine.

"Do you not have any hot water in your place?" Grania had asked once.

Sean had looked at her sharply. "Is that the kind of thing they say?"

"Who?"

"Mam and Dad."

"No, I was just wondering."

"They weren't complaining then? Saying I used the house as a hotel?"

"Why would they say that?" Grania looked troubled.

"It's all right, Grania, you are a funny little roly-poly," he said, punching her playfully on the arm.

People told Lizzie that she was a little star or a little gem but never a little roly-poly.

"You're dead lucky," Lizzy said to her over and over. "You're nearly as well off as an only child."

"Aw, come on," Grania protested. "You're the lucky one, the eldest of your family."

But Lizzie wouldn't be shaken. Grania had the house to herself, and no awful whining younger ones taking her clothes, coming into her room, reporting her to parents, sulking, having to be minded.

"And another thing, your parents have proper lives. I mean they're not always going on groaning and moaning about the family this and the family that. They didn't go mad or anything when your brothers and sister went away. I'm never going to be let go away. I'm going to be in my house until I'm an old, old woman." Lizzie was very dramatic.

"I think they moan and groan just as much as anyone's family," Grania said.

"But they're hardly ever there," Lizzie said enviously.

"They go out to work, but they come back." Grania was defensive.

"No, I mean they're never there together, sitting beside the fire droning on and on about the family. They're out on their own or with their friends."

Was this true? Grania wondered.

She didn't want them to be different to other people, Mam and Dad. Was it odd that they didn't sit beside the fire and talk?

She checked it out with a few friends from school.

Oh, it was desperate, their mothers and fathers never got out of the way, they sat and chose what television the family would watch, they went on and on about homework to be finished first, they had cups of tea, trays and biscuits and pints of beer, and you'd love a bit of peace, wouldn't you?

Grania wondered, would you love it all that much?

Her house was very quiet indeed. She was always delighted when Sean came back with his bags of dirty washing or Catherine came in with some fruit.

There was certainly no one sitting down around the fire to welcome them. Often Dad was out working late or Mam had gone to see what she called the Girls, who were really women as old as herself from the factory where she worked.

Maybe it *was* unusual, but Grania told herself she must not worry about it, she was always a bit of a worrier in her heart. Was she too fat, was she a bit slow in class, would boys ever fancy her, would she look better if she smoked like Lizzie did, or would she get like Catherine, trying a new cure every few months to try and give it up?

And Mam and Dad loved Grania, they must love her a lot or else why were they always planning things they would do when she grew up? She heard the phrase over and over. Not so much about holidays in America now, more about changes in the house.

Maybe they were thinking of giving her a flat of her own. She had read about rich people having this, a little apartment where you could come and go and still be part of the family.

There was a downstairs toilet; possibly they were thinking of putting in a shower and washbasin.

She didn't like to ask in case it looked greedy.

She heard Dad saying to one of his friends that when Grania was grown up all that would be settled.

Dad's friend had said gloomily that it would all cost a fortune and Dad had nodded and said it would be worth it.

Grania was pleased. Whatever it was would be great.

Sometimes she could hardly wait.

"Will I be grown up when I'm fourteen?" she asked her mother.

"Why do you say that?"

"Well, we often talk about when I'm grown up. I wondered would it be at fourteen."

"More sixteen I'd say." Her mother sounded wistful.

"Would you like me to grow up at fourteen?" Grania asked.

Mam was definitely sad today.

"You're a great child, you were never a moment's trouble to us, never. Do you know that?"

"Well, I must have been a bit of a nuisance, coming along so late when your family was grown up already." Grania felt very adult saying something like this.

Mam seemed surprised.

"What kind of talk is that?" she asked.

"It's what Lizzie says, Lizzie thinks it was a shock that I was born, she says you probably thought you were too old for having another baby."

"Lizzie's very wrong, as she is about a lot of things. We wanted you, we were mad for another baby."

"Did you pray for me?" Grania asked.

"Yes, well, I suppose we did, a bit, as well as—"

"Yes, I know what else you had to do."

"So anyway now you know you weren't an accident, you were what we both wanted to make our lives— well, to make them better."

"Were they not good, your life and Dad's life?"

Grania's eyes were open wide, she felt that her face was very round like people's faces are when they are reflected in a clean frying pan.

Sometimes you could actually feel rounder or fatter than others. She wondered was that something everyone else knew or only her own secret.

"They were okay, Grania, like everyone's life is."

Something stopped her asking if her arrival had done the trick and made them better.

Suppose they had said no.

"You know I'd say I'm nearly grown up, Mam," Grania said.

She hoped it would cheer her mother up.

"We thought sixteen, Grania, your dad and myself, we thought we'd agree you were grown up then."

"In some countries I could marry and have children at this age."

"Don't be in any hurry," Mam said.

Grania reported it all to Lizzie. They told each other everything.

"I can't understand it," Grania said. "First she said that they were delighted with me, then she said I wasn't to rush into getting married and having babies myself. It's not logical."

"Maybe she's going through the change of life . . . and just got very confused about everything." Lizzie was informed about such things.

"She was eighteen when she married, she'd be about forty-three now. That's not all that old."

"It's old enough to be confused, though," Lizzie said.

Dad didn't come home from work one evening. Grania was doing her homework at the kitchen table and waiting for him to come in the door.

"What could he be doing?" she asked Mam, who was sitting reading a magazine.

There was no supper ready for Dad or anything. Since they had a microwave now everyone cooked their own.

"He could be doing anything on earth," Mam said without raising her eyes from the pages.

"You and he aren't fighting, Mam?"

Her mother looked up. "No, we gave up fighting long ago. Truly."

Grania believed her.

"So everything's all right, is it?"

"As all right as it ever is for people."

Grania said nothing because she didn't want to hear any more.

Dad didn't come home four nights that week.

Her sister, Catherine, called on Mam's late night in the factory.

"Everything all right?" Catherine asked over and over.

But Grania closed her ears to the worry.

If she admitted it then it would become real.

"They're not upsetting you?"

Grania was shocked. "Of course not, they're fine, they were only saying the other day that their life was all right as it is for most people."

"But it's you I care about," Catherine said. "You can come to us anytime, Gerry says so too."

"Thanks," said Grania. "That's very nice of you both."

Patrick rang from America.

"You sure things are all right?" he asked.

For some reason that she didn't understand Grania told him, "Things have never been better. We all eat our dinner together, Mam, Dad, and I, and we tell jokes," she said.

"That's terrific," said Patrick.

She decided to go over to Lizzie's before Sean arrived.

Outside the house a girl stood looking up at the windows.

She was in her twenties, maybe someone come looking for Catherine.

She was very pregnant.

"Were you looking for Catherine?"

"No," the girl said. "Just looking, that's all."

She seemed a bit lost and sad, as if she was worried and couldn't make up her mind.

"Would you like to come in or anything?" Grania looked doubtful. "There's no one at home really, only me and I was going out to my friend."

The girl's eyes filled with tears.

"No, no, I'm sorry, it's stupid to come and stare, I'll go off now."

"Are you getting on the bus?" Grania was helpful. "There should be one in a few minutes."

"Don't be nice," the girl said, crying. "Whatever else you do, don't be nice," and she ran off lumbering with the great weight she carried in front of her.

At Lizzie's house Grania didn't tell any of this. She played games with Lizzie's little sisters and was very nice to them.

"I wish you were our sister, not Lizzie," said the younger one. According to Lizzie she was a total monster.

"I'd like to have had a younger sister. You see when I grow up there'll be no family left," Grania said, and she felt very cold suddenly.

Maybe this was what they had been waiting for.

Dad not coming home, Mam waiting, counting the time, the rest of the family asking was she all right. And the girl at the door, the girl crying and looking at the house. She had something to do with it definitely.

She must have come to look at the house where Dad lived and wondered was he ever going to leave it and come and live with her.

And Dad must have told her he would, "When Grania grows up."

Lizzie had been sent to tidy her room. Lizzie's mother said that Lizzie's room looked like those awful pictures you saw in a war zone. Grania went to help her, moving quietly, hanging up clothes.

"Is this an extra bed?" she asked as they cleared a surface.

"Yeah, it's a divan, you know that," Lizzie said.

Grania went on folding and sorting. Soon they had all the dirty clothes waiting for the washing machine and the clean ones hanging in a closet.

"Now, it wasn't too bad, was it?" Grania said. "Would there be a sheet or anything if I wanted to stay the night now and then?"

"But you only live two streets away." Lizzie was surprised.

"Sure, but I'd like to think that I had somewhere to go, you know, somewhere that wasn't a bar in New York or a mobile home or a place with people who have filthy clothes in Sean's flat."

"What's wrong with your home?" Lizzie's eyes were wide open.

"If you don't want me I have other friends at school, you know."

"Don't be stupid, of course I want you, but there *are* the awful awful gross children to take into consideration."

"They're okay, your sisters, don't keep going on at them like that. They're just like us only younger."

Lizzie looked at her, astonished.

"You've changed," she said suspiciously. "Did something happen?"

"Yes, I grew up. You know the way people do at different ages. Well, I've done it now."

She felt very calm and different somehow.

Lizzie went to her mother. Grania could hear her asking could Grania stay.

"The room's all tidy now, come and look at it," she begged.

"I know it is, of course she can stay, I was expecting she would soon."

"How did you know that?" Lizzie snapped, annoyed that her mother should have guessed something she hadn't.

"Well, Grania's growing up, you see, she'd prefer to have a place she can come to . . . you know."

"I know," said Lizzie in a voice that wasn't at all sure.

"My mother says it's fine." She came back with the news.

"Good, thanks a lot, I'll go home for my night things and some clothes for tomorrow at school."

"What'll they say at home?" Grania could see

Lizzie's face full of the uncertainty and anxiety she herself had felt until a short while ago, the feeling that the world was changing all around you and you weren't in charge of it.

"I think I'll just tell them a bit at a time," Grania said. "You know, they mightn't accept that I had grown up so quickly. They were expecting it a bit later."

"And will they be pleased, do you think?" Lizzie was still at sea.

"I think they'll be pleased as most people are about anything."

Grania used the words her mother had used.

She would probably speak like that a lot from now on.

MAEVE BINCHY

MAEVE BINCHY was born and educated in Dublin. She is the author of the bestselling books *Aches and Pains, Evening Class, This Year It Will Be Different, The Glass Lake, The Copper Beech, The Lilac Bus, Circle of Friends, Silver Wedding, Firefly Summer, Echoes, Light a Penny Candle, London Transports,* and *Tara Road,* as well as three volumes of short stories, two plays, and a teleplay that won three awards at the Prague Film Festival. She has been writing for *The Irish Times* since 1969 and lives with her husband, Gordon Snell, in Dublin.

ONE DAY WHEN WE WERE YOUNG

by Vincent Banville

The year Mikey became thirteen he began to
look at girls with a much less jaundiced eye
than of yore. Before that there had been his younger
sister, Nelly, but nothing much could be done about
her. She was a fact of life, like rainy days, school,
and the weekly bath in the tin tub in front of the
fire on Saturday nights: all to be gone through with
gritted teeth and the thought that nothing lasts forever.

And then there were Nelly's friends, gigglers in
dresses whose emotions could turn stormy for no reason at all and who fought with their nails and their teeth
instead of with their fists. When they tagged along—
"Keep an eye out for Nelly" was his mother's habitual
cry—they had to be included in all games: as gangsters'

molls, squaws, or holding the imaginary horses while the boys robbed the equally imaginary bank.

Mikey was part of the triumvirate known as the Three Mesquiteers, he invariably being the hero because he thought up the stories. Cecil Baxter, tall and pale as egg white, was his right-hand man, while Joey Malone, fat and roly-poly, was the bumbler of the group. In that particular year of 1955 they stepped in and out of their fantasy world a little less decisively, looking back over their shoulders more often, unwilling to let go of their youthful games completely but more and more aware of bigger boys' scorn and their own lack of certainty.

It all began really on the day they spied on the girls for the first time. It was Cecil's idea.

"Why're they always lagging behind?" he had asked as they jogged through the sagebrush—a field of thistles actually—up near the shelf of rock known as Maiden Tower. "Have you noticed? Once they complained about being left behind, now they're always hiding and dodging."

"What d'you mean, Cecil?" Joey had asked, his large moon face mirroring his ingrained perplexity.

"What do I mean, is it? How the hell do I know what I mean? They're up to something. I'll bet you a cat to a canary they're planning to ambush us."

They squatted down in the thistles to talk things over. Mikey was small for his age, but his natural intelligence caused the other two to look to him for guidance.

"I reckon they just can't keep up," he said. Then he added, "They're probably talking about girl things, like . . . like . . ."

"Like what, Mikey?" Joey asked.

"Well, dolls for a start."

"Babies, more like," Cecil Baxter said daringly.

The other two looked at him with their mouths open; then Mikey, nervous that control might be slipping away from him, said, "What's it matter anyway what they're on about? Good riddance to bad rubbish, I say"—although he couldn't help feeling uneasy at not really knowing what new interests were occupying the girls.

"Let's go back and have a look," Cecil suggested. "They're down in that hollow near Murphy's meadow."

The thought of actually doing something filled them with relief, and they retraced their steps in single file, Mikey first, then Cecil, then Joey taking up the rear as usual. The ground was humpbacked and gave natural cover, and they could hear the girls before they saw them. "Easy, men," Mikey commanded. They crouched down and proceeded on all fours.

At the rim of the hollow they carefully inched their heads up and over until they could see what was happening down below. In the heat of the sun the four girls had removed their dresses and were lying on the grass in their underwear making daisy chains. Their arms and legs gleamed stark and white against the greenness of the foliage and they laughed and talked as they worked. Clara Jowett, who was a Protestant and trailed an aura of mystery because of it, wore bright red panties, and her daisy chain was the longest where it snaked out in front of her.

"Cripes," Joey Malone breathed, the eyes starting out of his head, but the other two held their breaths and said nothing.

The sun went in behind a cloud and, as though a signal had been given, Mikey's sister, Nelly, looked up and saw them. "Boys," she yelled, startling the watchers on the rim even more than her companions. With hurried, crablike movements the boys wriggled their way backward; then, out of sight of those below, they ran helter-skelter as though being chased by the sheriff and his posse.

A cave in the western flank of Maiden Tower was their hideout, a raft of ferns securing the entrance. In the damp, greeny dimness of its interior they crouched to take stock, Cecil Baxter first lighting up the stub of a Woodbine cigarette and passing it ritualistically around.

"Them girls should be arrested," he announced with a sniff of disapproval. "They've no shame."

"Ah, you sound like yer ma," Mikey told him, the vision of Clara Jowett's bare rounded arm as she held the yellow-hearted flowers aloft in the sunlight still crystal clear in his mind.

Joey Malone looked puzzled, but then most things had that effect on him: Just as he was about to come to terms with one conundrum another trotted along to give him pause.

"Anyway," Mikey went on, "you'd see more down at the Blue Ponds. Some of them swimming suits only cover half what they're supposed to."

"It's not the same," Cecil pursued doggedly, and Mikey had to agree with him. There had been something about the girls in their underwear that had stirred a feeling, half apprehension, half delight, in his imagination. He wished he were back there, a silent observer of their strange rituals.

When they emerged blinking into the strong sunlight, Nelly was sitting alone on a rock moodily knocking her heels against its base. Obviously believing attack to be the best form of defense, she immediately accused them of being spies and worse: "It's no business of yours what we do," she said, before they even had a chance to taunt her; then, she burst into tears.

The boys went home along the railroad tracks, silent and rather downcast. They were at odds with themselves and one another, yet unable to grasp their feelings. Even Joey Malone, who was used to the impossibility of understanding most things, could sympathize with their feelings of disquiet.

That evening, still agitated by visions of Clara Jowett, Mikey took his bicycle and pedaled it out along the sea road, head down, legs pumping, the breath sawing in his throat. The sun was still above the horizon and it infused streaks of red and orange into the mackerel sky. The old bridge had barrels staggered along it to prevent motorists from speeding, and he zigzagged around them with abandon. He passed the Norman round tower, then the ruined castle to his left. Down below in the curve of the bay, fishermen in rowing boats trawled their nets for the salmon seeking upland rivers in which to spawn. Pausing on the crest of the rise and standing astride his bicycle, Mikey watched as the nets were pulled in, sensing rather than seeing the silver sheen and flash of the imprisoned fish. He knew their anxious flapping would avail them little, and he flinched when he heard the dull thuds as their heads were beaten against the sides of the boats.

He continued on, cutting inland through leafy caverns of trees where their foliage overhung the road. The declining sun still winked through the leaves, stabs of brilliance followed by spooky pockets of dimness. It was in his mind to do something new, something that hedged about it a certain danger. For as long as he could remember he had been warned against going to visit the old ruined house known as Lady Dane's: "It's too dangerous," his father was forever warning him. "The floors have given way, a wall could collapse . . ."

Earlier that summer they had gone out to the rundown estate on a family picnic, with a hired pony and carriage, jingling along the lane that led in under slick and oily-looking laurels, the pony's rump rising and falling comically. Mikey had been allowed to hold the reins, much to the chagrin of Nelly and his younger brother, Sean, and he had felt like a driver threading his stagecoach through dangerous territory.

Now he pointed his bicycle up that same lane, the wheels bumping and grinding over the ruts, his bottom raised in the air to avoid painful contact with the iron-hard saddle. A stream tinkled and slid over ocher soil to his right, and to his left scrub and bramble bushes formed an impenetrable barrier to the bank that rose steeply to cut off the sky.

There was an old water mill at the end of the way in, its wheel pitted and holed, the wood smooth and darkly gleaming through years of water washing over it. Weeds grew along its roof and a couple of sapling alders had taken root and were thriving.

Mikey dismounted and hid his bicycle in beside the wall and its overhang of bushes. The place was deserted, a quietness brooding over everything that was broken only by the odd trilling of birdsong. He made his way across the stream, fording it by means of the rocks that had been placed there for just that purpose. Farther on, he knew, the stream became a waterfall, but where he crossed it, it was still no more than a gliding murmur.

He pushed his way through ferns and banks of ragwort, stopping now and then to search for wild strawberries. There had once been an orchard and extensive gardens surrounding Lady Dane's, but everything was now overgrown and unkempt.

He fought his way through clinging brush until he had a view of the house. One entire side of it had

fallen in, the rooms vulnerable and exposed like draw-
ers in a bureau that had been carelessly pulled out and
vandalized. Once, on another visit with his father,
Mikey had found what he supposed was the skeleton
of a cat, and he'd wondered if some great catastrophe
had overtaken the house and its inhabitants. The discovery had caused him to back off in case he might
come across human remains.

Now he amazed himself by his audacity in pene-
trating so far, and wished that he had someone with
him. It was not his fellow Mesquiteers that he wished
for but Clara Jowett, she of the red panties and the
softly rounded limbs. He pictured the delight of an-
ticipation on her face as, safely standing on ground
level, she watched him pick his way over shattered
stone and shale, the raddled remains of the old
house's dying, and climb upward toward the slice of
deep indigo sky visible through the gaping hole in
the roof.

He knew that what he was doing was foolhardy, but
the knowledge only spurred him on. It was as if a
chasm had opened in front of him and, if he didn't
manage to get across to the other side, he'd be stuck
forever in solitude, while everything else he knew and
loved would journey on without him.

In places the stairs still remained, the wood

creaking and groaning under his tentative footsteps. Once, part of it fell away behind him, and he stood pressed to the wall while the masonry crashed and echoed eerily. A wood pigeon rose *whoo-whoo*ing, the flap of its wings tremendous in the stillness of the evening air. His heart thumped and he had to fight for breath, but the determination was still strong in him to go on.

He finally made it to a place just under the roof, but he was afraid to look down in case the enormity of his daring might overcome him. A firm-looking beam of wood poked out a little way from him, and he sidled around toward it until it was within reach. Carefully setting one foot down after the other, he inched along, then changed his mind and eased himself into a sitting position astride the beam. Again he moved outward, into a slanting ray of sunlight, and this time, when he plucked up the courage to look, he saw with a delicious shiver that he was perched high above the world, a watcher in the sky.

The exhilaration that gripped him was so sharp that it was like a stab of pain. This was daring to the limit, a madness that, if he ever got down, would remain with him forever. Looking below him, he could spy the waterfall, an expanse of trees, then farther out fields, the tremble of smoke from the chimney of a house half hidden, and the glint of the sea in the distance.

He stretched his arms out wide; if he were to flap them he would be able to fly, up, up, and away like Captain Marvel in the comics. He felt weightless, as if his body had dissolved and he had become as one with the air, but then the beam he was astride creaked and he was brought back to the realization that he was only mortal and in danger of falling if he didn't retrace his way and be quick about it.

Taking one last look downward, he saw a stirring of life in the brush below him. Lying in a grassy hollow were two people entwined, a pair of lovers oblivious of his regard. Many times in the past, himself, Cecil, and Joey had crept up on such couples, hooting and making fun of them in order to be chased, but now he felt a strange bond with the pair below him. That was himself down there, himself and Clara Jowett: It was so obvious to him that he could feel the tickle of the grass, the softness of the girl's body, the scent of her hair, and over him stole a warmth the like of which he had never experienced before, a pure shiver of sensation that was like a beginning and an end all rolled into one. In that moment he felt part of himself fall away with a whisper of regret that had in it the implication that it was saying goodbye forever. . . .

Later, riding home in the purple fall of twilight, he saw Clara Jowett strolling along the boardwalk beside the sea, and when he veered to salute her, she put out her tongue and called him a vulgar name.

VINCENT BANVILLE

VINCENT BANVILLE was born and educated in Wexford, Ireland. After receiving his B.A. and Higher Diploma from University College, Dublin, he taught secondary school in Nigeria for six years. His novel *An End to Flight* won the Robert Pitman Literary Prize. He is the author of five popular books about a streetwise fifteen-year-old called Hennessy, as well as novels for adults featuring Dublin private detective John Blaine. He lives in Dublin, where he is the crime fiction reviewer for *The Irish Times*.

SAYING GOODBYE

by Tony Hickey

The rain found the crack in the west-facing wall of the assembly hall of the St. Joseph's old school and began to drip onto the radiators by the exit to the yard.

To Martin the grayness and chill of the day were more like February than June and increased the bleakness of his surroundings.

By right he and his classmates should not have been in this assembly hall at all. They should have been in the long-awaited new St. Joseph's school but its completion had been delayed by industrial disputes and funding problems. It was now scheduled to open in September, when Martin's class would be out in the big, bad world, starting their adult lives. This meant that they would be the last group to have spent their entire teenage education years in these draft-riddled, creaky old premises.

There was talk in the town of turning the building into a community center. No matter how run-down it was, it would be nice to think of the old school still being used rather than just being left to become even more dilapidated.

Suddenly Martin realized that he was becoming sentimental about a place long past its sell-by date, where life had often been like serving a dull, monotonous prison sentence.

Conor, his best friend, would have had something sharp to say in response to such feelings. He always referred to the school as "the dump." Conor specialized in being sarcastic and world-weary, and as so often happens with close friends, he and Martin could not have been more different.

Conor's father owned the local butcher shop.

Martin's parents owned a small farm three miles outside the town and weren't pleased about Martin and Conor spending so much time together. Martin played dumb, pretending not to be aware of their disapproval.

But where was Conor right now?

Mr. Murphy, the school principal, was due in the hall at noon to make his farewell address to the senior class before the lead-up to their final exams.

It was an annual task that Mr. Murphy took very seriously. He would not look kindly on absentees especially if the absentee was Conor, whose sharp tongue had involved him in more run-ins with the school authorities than anyone else in the history of the school. Sometimes it seemed as if Conor was deliberately trying to provoke them into expelling him. No one, not even Katie, his longtime girlfriend, could reason with him when he got into one of these moods. It was best just to wait for things to cool down, to let Conor chill out.

Conor was lucky that the teachers, whom he described as "a bunch of creeps," were so patient with him. All they did was keep him back after school or make him stand in the corridor until Mr. Murphy encountered him on one of his rounds of inspection and verbally wiped the floor with him.

Martin had overheard one such telling-off. "You are a fool to yourself. You are your own worst enemy. You have more brains than anyone else in the school. You could do anything, become anything. Yet you waste your energies making a nuisance of yourself!"

And Conor was brilliant at anything he put his mind to. Two years ago he had been the only boy to be on every team in the school. Then he just threw it all away, failing to turn up for practice, behaving like a zombie when he was selected for a game.

The same was true of his academic work. He won the annual essay prize and never afterwards turned in another decent piece of creative writing. He developed the best French accent in the school, but when his class went on a trip to Paris, he spoke the language so badly that no one could understand a word he said.

Now he could be heading for another showdown with Mr. Murphy.

The clock clicked to five to noon. There was less than five minutes to go. Shane Lynch tapped Martin on the shoulder. "Where's Conor? Off canoodling with Katie O'Brien, I suppose!"

Martin and Conor had no time for Shane. He was always carrying bad news and making trouble. Martin was about to tell him to mind his own business when the door from the yard was flung open and there was Conor, soaking wet, no jacket, no sweater, his shirt stuck to his body, his hair standing on end.

"Hey, close that door!" someone yelled as the wind carried a flurry of rain into the hall.

"But of course," Conor said, as, with a bow and a flourish, he shut the door.

"He's drunk," Shane Lynch said, delighted. "Wow, is this going to be fun!"

Martin felt like punching the great, gangling nitwit, but Conor needed attention. He grabbed him and indicated to the fellows in the back row to make room for them.

Mr. Maher, the math teacher, and Mr. Ryan, the physics teacher, strode in from the main part of the school and took their places on the platform. They were the advance party, there to underline the solemnity of the occasion and to herald the imminent arrival of Mr. Murphy. They glanced around the hall, ready to correct any breach of etiquette.

"Just look at them!" Conor said. "Like two stuffed turkeys waiting for Christmas!"

A wave of laughter rippled out from his section of the hall. The two teachers immediately went on alert.

"Maybe I should say a few words on behalf of my classmates before Big Boss Murphy starts his spiel." Conor tried to stand, but Martin grabbed one of his arms while Bill Nolan grabbed the other. Conor struggled to get free. "Hey, what is this? Let go!"

Then he saw Shane Lynch staring at him with a mixture of excitement and fearful fascination. "What are you staring at, you great mindless blob?"

"He *is* drunk!" Shane said. "I was right."

"But you always are right, aren't you? Always right when it comes to getting people into trouble! Here!" With a show of strength that caught Martin and Bill off balance, Conor freed himself from their grip, fished an almost empty bottle of vodka out of his pocket, and offered it to the wide-eyed Shane.

"Are you crazy?" Martin grabbed at the bottle, but Conor twisted away and waved it at the fellows next to him. "Here's to St. Joseph's," he said. "This is the last time I'll ever be in this dump!"

"You're forgetting about the exams next week!" Martin tried once more to get the bottle away from Conor.

Mr. Maher stood up. "What's going on down there?" he demanded.

"Everything and nothing!" Conor replied. He let go of the bottle and Shane, with a reflex action, caught it. Then he stared at it as though it were a hostile alien and dropped it. It shattered with a loud bang when it hit the stone floor.

"Shane Lynch, what are you up to?"

Shane turned the color of strawberries. "Nothing, sir!"

"He dropped and broke a perfectly good bottle of vodka," Conor said with such mock solemnity that in spite of the seriousness of the situation, even Martin joined in the fresh outbreak of laughter.

Before either teacher could decide whether or not to take Conor seriously, Mr. Murphy, dressed in his best dark-gray suit, came into the hall and onto the platform. He wasted no time getting down to business. "This is a most solemn moment in your lives. Soon you will no longer be pupils of St. Joseph's."

Conor slumped against Martin and, pretending to be asleep, made a loud snoring noise. Mr. Murphy, without any alteration in his expression or voice, nodded to Mr. Maher and Mr. Ryan. The two men left the platform and started down the hall toward Conor.

All the other boys in the hall stared straight ahead, seeming to hang on to every word spoken by Mr. Murphy, scared that they might, for even the most innocent reason, catch the eye of one of the teachers and become the target of his anger. And both men were very angry that anyone, and especially a defiant brat like Conor Doyle, should so blatantly make fun of this occasion.

"Sit up! Please, sit up! Conor, for God's sake, sit up!" Martin tried to haul Conor into a sitting position while Bill kicked the shattered bottle out of sight under the chairs. "It's just for a few minutes! Then you can go and see Katie!"

"I won't be seeing Katie anymore!" Conor pushed Martin away as Mr. Maher leaned over Shane Lynch. "Leave the Blob alone! He didn't do anything!"

"Then who did?" Mr. Maher demanded.

"Who do you think?" Conor stood up. "It was me, of course."

Mr. Murphy momentarily abandoned his speech, but his expression remained calm. "Is there a problem back there?" he asked.

"It's all under control," Mr. Maher said.

"It most certainly is under control; totally and undeniably under control! In fact I think we should all rise and sing the school song!" Conor dodged every restraining hand and reached the far end of the row. He clapped and shouted to the school tune.

"St. Joseph's is our favorite dump,
To see it we'd go far!
And we would go farther yet
To see it burn like tar!
Yes, let it burn
Down to the ground,
See how the high flame leaps
As it brings to an end
The reign of all these creeps!"

Mr. Ryan sprinted round to catch Conor at the other side of the hall. Mr. Maher pushed past Bill and Martin. Conor ran as if to collide with Mr. Ryan. Then he changed direction and plowed through the center rows, scattering chairs and pupils in all directions.

The assembly hall was now in total pandemonium, yet Mr. Murphy seemed to remain quite unaffected. Conor paused for a second and briefly locked gazes with the headmaster. Mr. Murphy did not give the slightest flicker of recognition. Conor grinned in a way that could almost be described as admiring and kicked open the doors into the yard.

By the time the pursuing teachers had got through the confusion of upturned chairs and startled pupils, Conor was long gone into the rain.

Martin made as if to follow him. Bill said, "No."

"He needs help!"

"He'll ruin your life too!"

"Will everyone please return to their places?" Mr. Murphy resumed his speech as though it had never been interrupted.

It wasn't a bad speech, as such speeches go, with the usual phrases about honor, dignity, application, hard work, and being a credit to St. Joseph's. It ended with a reminder that a full-scale review for the coming exams would begin next morning.

"Please do not be late. These next few days are very important." Mr. Murphy nodded briefly, acknowledging the round of applause which Mr. Maher and Mr. Ryan had begun. Then everyone sang the correct words of the school song.

When the teachers had left the hall Shane Lynch

said, "That pig friend of yours could have got me expelled!"

"He saved you, so just shut up!" Martin said. He pulled the hood of his windbreaker over his head and ran across the yard onto the road. He hoped Conor would be waiting there for him. But he wasn't.

Nor was there any sign of him on the main street of the town. Instead all there was to be seen were four cars outside the supermarket and a donkey and cart outside the post office.

The donkey flapped its long eyelashes as Martin hurried past. A dog looked out of a doorway and wagged his tall. A cat on a damp window ledge arched her back, wanting to be stroked.

On the other side of the river was St. Mary's Convent School. It had the same deserted look as the main street. The girls were either still in class or had gone to lunch.

The thought crashed into Martin's mind that maybe Conor's behavior was because of a quarrel with Katie.

He sprinted down the side street to Doyle's butcher shop. The window blinds were down. The CLOSED sign was on the door. Martin rang the bell. Nothing happened.

He rang the bell again. A window above the shop

was opened. Conor leaned out and spoke in a clear, steady voice. "Are you alone? Mr. Murphy didn't send a posse after me?"

"You're not drunk? It was all an act?"

"You sound disappointed."

"Let me in out of this rain. I have to talk to you."

While Martin waited for Conor to open the door, the rain stopped as though it had been turned off. The sun burst through the clouds and gilded the street.

Conor looked at the brightening sky. "Do you think that could be called a ray of hope?"

Martin was in no mood for any more of Conor's attempts at humor. "What the hell is going on? Did you and Katie have a row? Is that why you tried to upset everyone at the school?"

"What happened there has nothing to do with Katie. It has to do with this place and all the places like it in this town."

To get to the upstairs living quarters they had to go through the shop, which was like a set from a horror film. Instruments for cutting up carcasses hung from hooks. A wooden block was stained with blood. Most sinister of all was the cashier's booth, into which a shape like a porthole had been cut to allow money to be paid. In the blueness of the light filtering through the blinds, the porthole looked like a headrest for victims of the guillotine. "Why isn't the shop open?"

"It's Monday." Conor replied. "According to tradition, butcher shops never open on Mondays. My old man sometimes forgets to open on Tuesdays as well."

"Is he sick?"

"Depends on what you mean by sick."

"I mean has he anything to do with your carry-on?"

"He has everything and nothing to do with what you call my carry-on!"

Upstairs the smell of the shop yielded to other smells, mostly cigarettes and beer. Stale air and dust hung over everything like an invisible veil. Conor laughed sardonically. "Not quite what you're used to, is it? I've tried to clean it, but my wonderful father just untidies it again."

"Why would he do that?"

"Revenge on my mother for walking out on him when I was three years old. You don't know about that?"

Martin had heard talk about Conor's mother from Shane Lynch and had pushed it to the back of his mind, dismissing it as another attempt by the Blob to cause trouble.

"In the beginning I used to hate her for leaving me.

I used to believe that she didn't love me but now I think she just couldn't bear to stay here a moment longer. If she had stayed on my account both of us would have been trapped. I've often wished that I could get in touch with her, but I don't know where she is. Of course I get angry about it all sometimes and go off the deep end. Then lately I've begun to see that all the trouble that I got into at school was a kind of rehearsal for what I did there today. And now I'm free of it."

"But you have only to put up with it for three more weeks! Then the exams will be over!"

"Mr. Murphy won't let me sit for the exams now. He can't, not without losing face."

"If you were to explain—"

"Explain what? This place? Explain that my father is still trying to get his revenge on my mother by making everything as ugly as he can for me? Anyway Mr. Murphy knows all this. That's why he's tried in his own way to make me face up to what he calls my full potential. Now I've thrown everything that he's tried to do back in his face."

"You can sit your exams at an examination center. They aren't school exams. They're state exams. No one blames you for what happened between your parents."

"Oh yes, they do! I've seen the light go out of your mother's eyes whenever she sees you and me together. How easy do you think it was for Katie to go out with me this last year? Anyway you're missing the point. I don't want to do the exams at all. By not doing them, I've at last started burning my bridges. If I pass the exams I'm stuck here forever."

"But where will you go?"

"America. I want to dance in the California sunshine for a while, live that life of sun and sand like they do in those beach movies."

"Those movies are fantasies!"

"That doesn't mean I can't make them come true for a while."

"But how will you get there?"

"With this." Conor rummaged through cushions on a couch and pulled out an envelope stuffed with pound notes. "The last ten days' takings in the shop. Dad was too drunk to go to the bank. I've left a note on the cash register explaining what's happened to the money. I regard it as my inheritance—no further demands to be made! By the time he's figured out what's going on, I'll be in America."

"You'll need a visa."

"I got one of those new ones they were advertising."

"I don't believe you!"

"It's true. When I didn't turn up for school before Christmas—"

"You said you just didn't feel like going to school—"

"I went to Dublin to the embassy."

"But you'd need documents and signatures—"

"I managed that."

"By forging your father's name?"

"Look, the less you know, the less you can tell after I've gone. Just believe me when I say I'm off, out of this place." He stuffed the envelope of money inside his shirt and pulled on a sweater. Then he reached behind the couch and picked up a red holdall. "My father could wake up any minute now and start looking for his breakfast. It's not a pretty sight! If you'll take my advice you won't hang around to witness it." He pushed past Martin. "Make sure you close the shop door. We don't want stray dogs getting in to chew on the meat."

Martin caught up with Conor on the river path that led to the road to Dublin. "What will you do when the money runs out? You've no qualifications of any kind. You won't be able to get a job!"

"Friends there will arrange everything for me."

"What friends?"

"You don't know them."

"How can I not know them?"

"All this talk isn't going to change anything! Just accept that I'm leaving here."

"And our friendship means nothing? You've been planning this for months and never said a word?"

"I didn't say a word because I wasn't sure if I had the guts to do what I had to do to end it all."

"You make it sound like suicide."

"It's the opposite of suicide. It's the start of a new life." He turned away but not quickly enough to hide the uncertainty in his eyes.

A group of girls from the convent passed by. Martin said, "Do you know where Katie O'Brien is?"

They were startled and paused before the tallest of them said, "She's down at the burger bar."

"Then do me a favor. Tell her that Conor and Martin have to see her at once. Please. It's very important!"

The girls hesitated, trying to decide if the message was a trick to get Katie alone.

"Please!" Martin repeated the word as firmly as possible. "I'd go myself but there isn't time. Tell her to follow the river path until she finds us."

The girls exchanged glances and came to a decision. "Okay, but you'd better be telling the truth when you say it's important."

"It is important. I promise you that it's important."

The girls ran back toward the town.

"That was stupid," Conor said, without turning around. "It won't change anything. You just don't get it, do you?"

"Maybe I don't 'get it' because I thought friends confided in friends and didn't just go away like this. It's as if I never really knew you."

"Maybe I never knew myself until lately. Maybe I'm meeting myself for the very first time. Maybe I didn't tell you because I'm jealous of the fact that you belong here in a way that I never could. I could stay here forever and just be rubbish. I could go away for twenty years and come back and still be rubbish. But you love this place. You love your parents' farm. You love the mountains and the rivers and the lakes. You'll do well in your exams. You'll go to agricultural college and get a degree. You'll get married, have kids, buy more land. You won't even notice how dull your life is. Well, that kind of life is not open to me even if I wanted it."

"You're trying to pick a fight so that you won't feel guilty about what you're doing."

"If that's what you want to think, then go ahead and think it!"

"There are just a few more weeks, Conor, just a few more weeks until the exams are finished! It's not too late to put the money back and tear up the letter. You can come and stay at the farm until the exams are over."

"Your mother would love that!"

"She'd say yes if I told her how important it is."

"You're not making it easy for me."

"I don't want to make it easy for you!"

They were almost at the bridge where the road to Dublin began when they heard Katie call their names. Conor pushed Martin into the ditch and ran toward the road.

Martin scrambled out of the tangle of brambles as Katie drew level with him. "Are you all right?"

"Yes, but we have to stop Conor. Did he tell you that he was going away?"

"Where to?"

"America!"

"He's winding you up!"

Conor was on the bridge now. He looked back at them and waved. A bus swung around the corner and stopped when he held out his hand. Within seconds the road was empty once again.

Martin glanced at his watch. "That bus will stop at Barretstown. If there was some way we could get there—"

"And do what? Drag him off the bus?"

"You don't care what happens to him?"

"Of course I care! When he told me yesterday that he didn't want to see me anymore, I couldn't believe it. It was like a bolt from the blue. I thought I was being dumped, but now it occurs to me that it was his way of saying goodbye."

"But how can he be going to America? He says friends of his are going to find him a job. He doesn't have any friends in America."

"There's Paddy Halligan, who came home on a visit last December. Conor went out driving with him a few times. They even went to Dublin."

"Dublin?" Conor said. "He went there to get a visa just before Christmas. Paddy Halligan is old enough to be Conor's father. He might have helped by pretending to be his father. But why would Paddy Halligan help Conor to run away?"

"Maybe he's sorry for him." Then Katie paused and gazed in the direction the bus had taken. "Unless, of course, there is more to the friendship than we know. I only found out by chance that he was spending time with Paddy when he was supposed to be at school. He said nothing at all to you?" She pushed back her long blond hair, and for the first time, Martin saw how truly beautiful she was with her clear, creamy skin and pale green eyes.

"If Paddy Halligan is involved then he's just an escape route for Conor."

"That could be wishful thinking on your part. And on my part as well." Katie sighed. "It's not always easy to recognize the truth . . . especially when it's presented to you suddenly like this. Maybe life is like that sometimes."

"Like the way the weather suddenly changed a few minutes ago? Conor tried to make a joke about that, calling it a ray of hope. But none of this is a joke."

Katie smiled sadly. "Maybe he was trying to be kind to us. Maybe it was his way of . . . of relieving us of the responsibility of being his friends." She looked at Martin. "We won't have to defend him when word gets out about what he's done."

Martin saw the sense of what Katie had said. And he remembered Bill Nolan's words: "He'll ruin your life too!"

"I think word might already be out about him." There was so much left to be said and Martin wasn't sure how to continue the conversation. "I hope I didn't frighten you by sending those girls for you."

"Well, maybe a bit. I guess that I was afraid for a moment that Conor had done something stupid." She paused and once more looked down the empty road.

"He was really setting us free of him. I'm sure of that now."

"You sound as though you don't expect to ever see him again."

"He's gone. I have to face that fact." Suddenly she seemed older.

"There are other people in the world."

"Do you mean other fellows? Of course there are. If this was a movie you and I would suddenly realize that we were made for each other. But the truth is that we might never have even spoken to each other if it hadn't been for Conor."

It was Martin's turn to smile sadly. "Yeh, you're right."

"I'm going to be late for my music lesson."

They walked back toward the town. They both knew that soon there would be questions from parents, teachers, and friends. They would have a difficult time convincing people that they hadn't known in advance what Conor had been planning to do.

Martin also sensed that it would not now be possible for him just to accept the future that had been outlined for him that day by Conor. Conor had somehow managed to make him question every idea he had ever had.

He glanced at Katie and sensed that she was also

thinking how Conor would always be in her mind. He imagined how years from now, when they met on visits home from faraway places, the first thing they would talk about would be Conor. They would wonder what had happened to him. Yet they hadn't even realized that they had been saying goodbye to him.

But then *goodbye* was just a word. It didn't wipe out the past. It just divided it into sections.

TONY HICKEY

TONY HICKEY was born in Newbridge, County Kildare, and spent most of his childhood there. Since then he has lived in Dublin and London and traveled extensively in Europe and America. He has many TV, radio, and screen credits as a writer, critic, and dramatist. His twenty-fifth book for children is *Granny Green, Flying Detective;* other titles include *Castle of Dreams,* the Matchless Mice series, the Flip 'N' Flop series, and *Brian the Leprechaun.* Tony Hickey is a cofounder of the Children's Press and a member of the Writers in Schools Scheme and is on the board of directors of the Irish Writers Centre, Dublin.

ON THE VERGE
OF EXTINCTION

by Peter Cunningham

Extinct? I laugh aloud. They'll never be extinct, not as long as I can hear their call, as clear and distinct as I can still hear Masters's voice. The notion! I laugh again, a cackle I imagine from the look the little black-haired nurse, the one with the bad breath, shoots me. She's never forgiven me the fact that I can read without glasses, a woman of my age.

Not that I do much anymore. My elder sister read all of Dickens again before she died at ninety-two. I'm sure that if another story by Dickens had been discovered she would have made the necessary adjustments; but none was and off she went. Radio is more to my liking. It's from my bedside radio that I heard this proposition about the corncrakes, those wonderful birds, being on the verge of extinction, this suggestion that made me laugh.

I laugh because I remember the corncrakes as being so vivid—the opposite to extinct—I remember everything that happened at that time. I was twelve. From the landing outside my bedroom at the top of the stairs, it was possible to look down through the stairwell, through the curling mahogany loops made by the banisters, and behold the tunnel up which all the noises from the floors below traveled with such facility. Noises of the men coming in from the fields for their tea, the kitchen women churning butter. My room was like a way station through which all the sounds had to pass. My elder sister had the less noisy room next to mine because of her age. She was thirteen. Then there was the guest room, and the bathroom, and finally the room of our parents. Once in there nothing whatsoever could be heard. But from my room I heard everything, not just from below but at those times when it was assumed I was asleep: the unrelenting monotone of my father, deep and sawlike, and then, when that sound ceased at last, my mother's sobs, leaking out beneath their door like a river of pain.

My father went off on two-day trips of cattle buying, to those parts of Ireland where beasts were wintered on porous limestone and then sold on to farms like ours, deep loamy farms with lush, fattening summer meadows. It was on those evenings that Masters always called.

When I think of Mother, now just a fading name on a tombstone, I think of a pretty, brown-headed woman on those summer nights. I think of someone associated with flowers, bearing them indoors in basketfuls, or arranging them, or braiding them into her wavy hair. Color and scent, is what I remember. Of roses and orange blossom. Of lavender and sage and woodbine that from June onward grew in such profusion beside our lake. I can still hear her lighthearted voice, and in the early evening, which I now know was the time she savored because he had yet to arrive, in this anticipatory hour, the sound of her whistling, a strictly forbidden activity in our father's company.

My sister and I were given early kitchen tea on those evenings and sent upstairs to our rooms. A book of pressed flowers—what has become of it?—preoccupied my sister. I lay in my nightdress on the summer quilt, watching the changing evening light through the drawn curtains and listening, listening, door an inch ajar, to the world I had left downstairs. Much later, when Masters's trap eventually rolled away on its reassuring wooden wheel rims and the darkness had become truly established, I still lay awake, treasuring what I had heard that evening, the rare, fond words, the bursts of laughter, and then gradually I ebbed into sleep listening to the cries of the corn-crakes.

Once a year Mr. Henderson, our clergyman, was asked for tea, although our father hated clergy of any hue and sat for the duration of the visit scowling.

"Mr. Masters has bought a new machine for bundling hay," observed the clergyman brightly.

My sister and I drank in every detail. When Mr. Henderson had left we would spend days mimicking the way he held his cup—his fingers a balletic attach-ment—the way his bald head sweated, the way you could, if you bent to stroke our cat, see his stomach hairs in the eyehole beneath his waistcoat.

"Hmmph," said our father.

"He's the go-ahead young man," plowed on our man of God. "A bright spark, no doubt, is young Mr. Mas-ters."

I noticed Mother busying herself with the plates of scones and gingerbread, two little roses of colors bud-ding in her cheeks.

"Hmmph."

"All he needs now is a wife," concluded Mr. Hender-son. "A wife and a little brood." The clergyman's tongue patrolled his upper lip in search of a stray crumb. "Can I say without fear of contradiction that I have never tasted gingerbread the like of what this house offers?"

Mother allowed her blushes to flower out of all proportion to this compliment. Across the room our father's dark eyes simmered with resentment, for he knew that Mr. Henderson would go home with a basketful of gingerbread made specially for him by the kitchen and he considered this the central purpose of the clergyman's visit.

After the summer a tutor came daily up the mile of our drive and gave us lessons. Once, on a dark day in November when the oil in our lamps had run out, this teacher brought my sister and me for what he termed an educational walk in the apple orchard. We heard voices as we neared the wall, one voice low and familiar to my ears, the other shrill. Suddenly Mother ran out from the orchard, hand clutched to her face. We stared after her, mute. Then out came our father, his mouth trembling. He looked at us as if through a dark glass. Then he walked away and never once turned back. That evening as I lay in bed, downstairs I heard Mother explain to the women in the kitchen how she had bruised her face when her horse had ducked at a shadow behind the apple orchard and thrown her to the ground.

Masters lived alone in a big house over the hill,

about two miles away. If I climbed the trees on our front lawn, I could see the tips of the trees in Masters's. I whispered this observation to Mother, anticipating the gentling effect it would bring to her features. Her smile to me was full of love, and it bound us with our womanly secret.

Our father went away at first light one day, and that evening Masters came. I still do not know how he knew those days. He too was a farmer, so he would have been aware of the dates of the big fairs in the West. The house had burst with summer's scented blooms from early morning. Mother whistled, and played the piano, and even sat us down, me and my sister, and sang with us from a sheet of music. The three of us had sung, for we all knew that Masters would soon arrive.

He did, earlier than usual. He had flowers—more flowers!—for Mother and to my sister and me he each presented a cowslip. I wondered why I had not noticed before how his fair hair shone so, or how his eyes could be so blue, eyes that never for a moment left Mother as she fussed over us at tea, and teased out the flounces on my dress, and furiously brushed my sister's hair, as if to pause even for a moment would impel her to reciprocate his attention. We were sent to bed on the dot of eight, my sister with buttercups for her book, picked at the lake for her by Masters, myself in the grip of undying love.

Then, on the hinge of sleep, as corncrakes gave voice although it was not yet dark, I heard the sound of a steam car on the avenue. Voices from outside. The front-door bolt drawn over and the door swinging open. Our father's voice. Something about a train breaking down. And Masters, then, quietly bidding them goodnight. His wheel rims, no longer reassuring, biting down the avenue. Much later, when it was deep night, crockery smashed downstairs. Next morning, when we got up, Mother had already gone away for a holiday to her aunt who lived twenty miles distant.

After that, Masters never came. I could have asked Mother why, or when he was coming next, but I never did for I knew to do so would bring her pain. That did not stop me yearning for him, of course, not alone because I loved him deeply, which I did, but because I loved Mother even more.

Then the day came round again for Mr. Henderson and the kitchen women doubled up on gingerbread and our father could be heard to mutter darkly about scroungers who wore the cloth. At the last moment our father was called out by the men to help them with a bullock drowning in the lake. We exchanged smiles with Mother as the clergyman stuffed himself with egg sandwiches and spotted dog and hot scones on which country butter and whipped cream jointly melted.

"Tell me," he sighed gravely during an interval of repose, "does anyone ever see young Mr. Masters at all?"

Mother did not blush, but her eyes widened in a way they never would have had our father been in the room.

"Never comes to church anymore," said Mr. Henderson grimly.

She gasped, "Is he . . . left?"

"Can't be. I see men going to work there. In my book it can't be good for a young man like that living alone. I can't understand it. Ah well." Mr. Henderson's eyes took stock of the full plates and silver trays before him. He let out a mild belch. "Did I ever tell you, m'am, how highly I rate your gingerbread?"

Never, all that summer, despite our father's many trips, did we see Masters. Nor did he come during that winter or the following spring. And when next summer arrived and we made hay, my sister and I rode on the backs of the horses, wide as gondolas. They said it was the best summer of all time, that the hay would last a generation. Even the normally wet parts of our land went dry and we cut the grass off it, something no one could ever remember happening. But as if he could make only problems even from good fortune, our father said the hay would go to rot for want of shed space, and so in July he set out on a trip which would last three days, up to the very north of the country where men put up sheds for half the price they did near us. We stood out on the step before breakfast as the steam hackney came for him and he drove away, somber as an undertaker, down through his fields either side his avenue where teams of men and horses were already toiling to bring in the rare treasure.

I awoke that night with a start. The dusk had leached the evening light so that certain patterns on my curtains, those of flowers and wild grasses, remained etched in suspension against the frame of the window. What had awoken me was the voice of Masters, but it could not have been Masters's voice, for he had not come for over a year, or if it was he, then none of the usual, happy fuss that always preceded his arrival had been in evidence. And another reason it could not be Masters was the source of the voice I could hear, which came not as usual up the stairwell, but from the guest room along the corridor.

"I can't. I can't."

Caught in my throat that my sister would hear Mother, unaccountably jealous for our shared secret, I opened my door.

"He's a beast."

I knew who Masters meant. I knew.

"I can't leave him."

"Then you'll kill me."

"Oh dear God. Oh dear, dear God, help us."

I knew as I went back to bed and cried myself to sleep, I knew that the corncrakes too had heard the sadness in our house and understood the grief of love, for just as I was crying, so were they.

We saved all our hay and drew it into the biggest shed in the county, put up by journeymen who smoked pipes and worked twenty hours a day, most of it, to our father's intense but impotent disapproval, with their chests bared.

Throughout that August we heard talk of schools; our father had inspected several institutions for young ladies during his trip up north earlier that summer. It was a fresh matter for contention between our parents and often over meals the rancor that he had previously allowed to seep out only by night now burst out too in daylight.

I clung to the hope that we could always live there, that we were young ladies already, but neither my sister nor I ever had the courage to voice these hopes to our father, and Mother, we knew, was already grieving our departure. A man and a woman came by, he in a tall hat, she with little pale eyes I didn't trust. We were brought in and presented to them and I heard the woman tell our father that we would "do very nicely," as Mother sat over near the piano, her eyes reddened.

Everything suddenly rushed toward a day in early September. Our new clothes were ticked off on lists and packed into trunks with brass padlocks. The night before we left, lying on my bed after tea, I wondered would I ever lie there again. And then the corncrakes started. They were more in number and greater in volume than I had ever known. And although I associated their calls with great happiness, that night their cries filled me only with foreboding. I don't know what hour it was when I heard, first a carriage on the drive, then the totally out-of-place voice of Mr. Henderson, the clergyman. I knew, then, although I did not yet understand why, that I had been right to be afraid.

"Terrible thing, terrible thing," came his urgent voice up the shaft outside my room. "I cut the poor man down myself."

Mother's tears followed Mr. Henderson's departure, then her screams. Our father's shouts. I heard her come upstairs and go into the guest bedroom. Later, our father, his voice thick, called her from the hall, but she would not answer. He went into their own room and banged the door so hard that the whole house shook. Next morning she alone saw us off. And when we came home three months later, not to our farm but to the house of our aunt twenty miles away, Mother was far happier in this new household. But she would never again be as pretty as in those days when Masters was expected, and although we remained close until she died in her eighties, I never mentioned Masters to her, not that I had to, because we both knew, as we had always known, that he'd brought something rare into our lives.

So the notion I just heard on my radio that the corn-crake is on the verge of extinction in Ireland makes me laugh. There's nothing extinct about the corncrake. You can't extinguish a bird like that, with all its wisdom and canny intuition. Makes me wonder about those experts on the radio. If that nurse comes by again I'll pretend that I was laughing at a dream.

PETER CUNNINGHAM

PETER CUNNINGHAM is from Ireland's Southeast. His novels have been published in ten countries. His latest novel, *Consequences of the Heart*, was short-listed for the prestigious Listowel Writer's Prize and is available from Farrar, Straus & Giroux. He lives near Dublin.

A HEADSTRONG
GIRL

by Ita Daly

Every morning before breakfast Orla walked to the
extreme tip of the island. It was the best part of
the day, before the others had got up, when she had
the world to herself, the sweep of sky and sea with
only the occasional seagull winging down to say hello.
Orla loved the island. Stretched out on the scratchy
grass with her chin edging over the rim of the world,
she could look out on the vastness of the Atlantic
Ocean. Apart from an outcrop of rock to her east there
was nothing between her and America, out there
somewhere some three thousand miles away.

Every morning at this time Orla told herself that
she was coping very well. She hadn't called home since
the initial call on her arrival two weeks ago. She had
stuck it out and now she had only one more week of

being surrounded day and night by other teenagers, by endless giggling and squabbling and silly chattering in two languages.

Because she was seventeen Orla had been placed in one of the senior houses. Officially no English was allowed here because everyone was supposed to speak only Gaelic, the Irish language. All the other girls had spent previous summers in a Gaeltacht college, a rite of passage for most Irish teenagers—and an opportunity to learn a lot more interesting things than Irish irregular verbs.

When the other girls in the house found out that this was Orla's first Gaeltacht visit they set about telling her how to get around the rules. They weren't allowed to smoke or drink, so likely locals had to be picked out who would act as messengers. You had to be indoors by ten every night but it was easy enough to get out a window to meet a boy once the *bean an tí*, the housemother, and her husband were safely asleep. (Assignations never took place before two in the morning anyway, when the moon was well up and all the hardworking natives in bed.)

As for speaking Irish, nobody paid any heed to that rule. All you had to do was be alert so that when a member of the college staff loomed into sight you could quickly switch.

Orla hadn't come to improve her Irish; she was here

because her parents had said she must come and because she knew, much as she would like to deny it, that they were right. At seventeen she had little knowledge of the world of other kids her age. Every day at four o'clock she escaped from her school to return to the safety and tranquillity of her family. She had no friends, never went to parties, avoided all places where other kids gathered.

"I understand," her mother had said, taking her hand. "But you may have to leave home this time next year. You'll be finished school by then and you may have to choose a university outside Dublin. Besides, we won't always be here, Orla."

So Orla had chosen the Gaeltacht college on Inisheer.

Inisheer was the smallest of the Aran Islands, lying off the West Coast of Ireland, out from Galway Bay. Orla liked the idea of its remoteness and the fact that none of the kids from her school were likely to go there. They preferred to go to the Kerry Gaeltacht, where Mr. O'Flaherty, the most popular Irish teacher, came from. She thought she could put up with three weeks, even though it meant mornings spent in class, afternoons playing games together or swimming, evenings together also and, finally, sleeping in one of the houses, at least six students to a house.

Orla pulled herself up from the wet grass, stretched,

and turned her back on the Atlantic. The others would be just getting up now, hanging on in bed till the last minute. They thought she was mad, heading off into the morning mist each day when she could have snuggled down, enjoying an extra hour's sleep. In general they thought she was a bit odd, and Orla knew they were right. At school this didn't matter anymore. People were used to her and they left her alone. Here, things were different. After two weeks the others were still interested in her and Orla dreaded Sally McKeon's cool, amused gaze every time she sat down opposite her at the kitchen table. Sally was the ringleader in the house: confident, extroverted, always the first to break a rule or take on a dare.

A bit like I was myself, Orla thought ruefully, before it all happened and before Siobhan went away.

She headed down the little road leading to her house. It was a rough, stone-strewn path that wound between the little fields, dipping and rising with the stony contours of the island. By now fires had been lit in many of the houses and she could smell turf-smoke on the air along with sea and the gentler scent of wildflowers. Despite the constant rain, this place was a sort of paradise. If I could live here on my own, Orla thought, if I could run away, I could be happy.

She had been running away for the last five years.

And she had been running so fast that she had turned into another person. Only when she looked at Sally did her memory of her old self surface: twelve years old, bold as brass, walking arm in arm with Siobhan, careless, ogling the boys on her first day in her new school. Within a week her life had totally changed and had never been the same since. First there was the illness, but she had come through the operation. Then there were the long weeks of chemotherapy when she sometimes wished she had died. Next came the loss of Siobhan, who had been her best friend since they were four. Siobhan's father had got a job in Brussels and the whole family moved while Orla was still undergoing treatment. Finally there was her return to school, where all the other first-year students had already made their friends, and where Orla found herself friendless, timid and, under her silky brown wig, totally bald.

This was Orla's secret, which she hugged to herself. At first it hadn't been too bad because the doctors had assured her that once the chemotherapy was over, her hair would grow back. Every morning she had stared at her skull in the bathroom mirror, searching for signs of new hair. But as month followed month Orla began to despair. Now, when she thought of herself, she saw only baldness. She saw herself as deformed, a freak. A pariah. And the fact that nobody knew about her deformity only made things worse, for every minute of every day she lived in fear that others would discover her secret. So she rejected the friendliness of her classmates, avoiding situations where her secret might be discovered. The doctors could offer no explanation as to why her hair did not grow and still they told her that it would, eventually, if she just gave it time.

But Orla had given up hope. She knew now that she would always be bald. These days she didn't even let her mother see her bald head. She locked her bedroom door before she took off her wig at night and, gripping the edge of the dressing table, forced her eyes upward to the shiny surface of her skull. Often, there in the privacy of her own room, she found herself blushing with shame. She knew that she would never get married, never even have a real relationship with a boy. She imagined what it would be like to be standing in the moonlight in somebody's arms. He would kiss her, kiss her again with greater passion, reach up to stroke her hair and then feel it shift under his fingers.

Never. She would die a bald virgin. At least that way nobody would get a chance to laugh at her or pity her.

So she gathered her courage and faced life, but the effort changed her. She hated other teenagers, she hated doctors, but most of all she hated God. When she was thirteen she had sometimes wondered if God really did exist. Now she was sure that He did and she imagined Him peering down at her through the clouds and sniggering at her baldness. Having a laugh. He'd done it just for His own amusement.

Orla observed other kids with contempt. Noisy, attention-seeking, stupid, all pretending to be having such a great time. And if anything, the girls were worse than the boys. All that kissing and screaming when they met a friend. All that giggling when some boy made some stupid remark in class.

And on Inisheer she couldn't get away from them. The house she was staying in must be the noisiest on the island. It was the biggest, the only one offering the single room that Orla's mother had stipulated.

"Say I'm allergic to perfumes," Orla had suggested, "then they won't risk putting me in with anyone else."

I may be bald, Orla told herself, but at least my brain cells are functioning. Now as she approached the house the little fox terrier came out to greet her. He jumped up and down in delight, trying to lick her hand. Orla bent to pat him, overcome by a rush of self-pity. Her only friend on the island—this little black-and-white dog. But she quickly shook her head to clear away these thoughts and went in to face the others.

They were all seated round the table while the *bean an tí* doled out cornflakes from a giant-sized carton. Everyone claimed to hate the food they got here but Orla had noticed that they ate everything that was put in front of them. The one thing she simply could not swallow was the milk, which tasted so much stronger than the milk at home.

"Straight from the cow," Sally had said on their first morning. "Just the thing to put hairs on your chest."

Orla knew that this was just an expression but she had felt Sally's eyes resting on her as she had said the words. From that moment Orla feared Sally. She sensed Sally's interest in her, which grew as Orla remained immune to her, refusing to fall under her spell like all the others. As Orla kept to herself Sally's attitude became more thoughtful, her gaze meeting Orla's and resting there, appraisingly, until Orla was forced to look away. Orla could almost see her brain ticking over: What's with that weirdo, what makes her behave the way she does?

The *bean an tí* now beckoned Orla to a vacant place at the end of the table, handing her cornflakes and two slices of toast.

"I'm off to collect the eggs," she said in Irish, smiling round the table.

As soon as the kitchen door was closed the girls began to chatter in English. Sally, from the top of the table, stared down at Orla. "Pissing again, is it?"

Orla nodded.

"I'm fed up with this place. It's supposed to be summer and it hasn't stopped raining since we arrived. Well, I'm definitely not going to class today. I only washed my hair last night and can you imagine the state of me at the *ceilidhe* tonight if I have to walk to and from class in that downpour?"

Orla avoided the *ceilidhes,* the evening gatherings where they were supposed to learn Irish dancing. The dancing was fun but Orla couldn't risk being swung round by some boy in case her wig came off. Logically she knew that this wouldn't happen but that didn't stop her worrying about it. It was easier to just not go. Anyway, nobody but the younger kids was interested in the dancing. The *ceilidhes* were really an opportunity to get off with some fellow; to put your eye on someone, get him to walk you home, then arrange to meet him after curfew for a proper smooch. Every success or failure was dissected at breakfast the following morning. Some of the girls had already found boyfriends but not Sally, who declared herself to be "strictly interested in one-night stands."

Orla didn't believe her. She had a feeling that Sally was getting a bit desperate, wearing more makeup each day, making more noise at every meal. Orla was sure that she had been interested in David Buckley, a tall, blond boy from Sligo that everybody fancied. After the first week he had started going out with Emma Brown, whom Sally referred to as Miss Twinkletoes because of her ease at learning the new steps in Irish dancing. Sally could be a lot more vicious about Emma when she'd had a couple of cans of hard cider, although she was always careful to be sweet as pie to her face.

"Hey Orla," Sally suddenly called down the table. "Is your hair naturally wavy?"

Orla froze, her spoon halfway to her mouth. Like a rabbit caught in the glare of headlights, she couldn't move, just sat there helplessly, waiting for Sally to move in for the kill.

For this was it. Sally had figured out Orla's secret and would expose her now, any second, as they all sat round the breakfast table.

Gradually the chattering died as the others, alerted by Orla's tense stillness, turned to stare at her.

Someone said, "I think she's going to faint, look at the color of her."

Then, as from a great distance Orla heard Sally's voice. "Look, I'm sorry if you think I'm being nosy. I only asked because I thought that you've got the same sort of hair as me but yours never seems to go fuzzy in the rain—that's all."

Orla felt the blood surging inside her head and her heart beating, thumping against her ribs. Did Sally intend to play with her, to prolong the torture?

"I—" she began but her voice came out in a squeak. "I—"

And then she was saved as the *bean an tí* came bustling back into the kitchen. She laid a basket of brown and white eggs on the table. "They're laying well, the creatures," she said in Irish, holding up an enormous egg for their inspection. "And I've the best news for you girls. I met Mairtín Andy back from lobster fishing and he said that the sea is like a pond out by the Black Headland. Now that's a sure sign that the weather will take up, it never fails. I'd say the summer is here at last."

As if on cue the kitchen was flooded with a brilliant shaft of sun.

"Sunshine." Sally jumped up from the table and ran over to the window. "I'd forgotten what the sun looked like. Just look at that sky—blue. Blue-est. I cannot believe that this is Inisheer."

As the day progressed the temperature rose. Jeans and sweatshirts were discarded for the shorts and T-shirts that had remained folded in suitcases for the past two weeks. Sitting just inside the classroom window, Orla felt her spirits rise with the temperature. Despite what had taken place at breakfast, she felt her body expand and relax. She stretched her neck to look out at the patchwork of little stony fields, with a corner of the Atlantic just visible, twinkling in the bright light, inviting her in.

Just before they broke up at one o'clock their teacher announced, "There will be swimming this afternoon at *An Trá Bán*. But don't dare go near any of the other beaches," she warned. "There are very dangerous currents round this island and the *Trá Bán* is the only safe place to swim."

They hardly waited for her to finish as they began to tumble out of the school. Orla found herself being pulled along by Sally, who had taken her by the hand.

Sally rounded up her troops. "Are we all here? All the girls from our house? Right. A can of cider and my new lipstick for whoever's changed into their shorts first. And if I win—which I intend to—you lot will have to keep me in smokes for the rest of my stay here."

She lined them up on the dusty road. "On your marks, get set, go."

Nine girls began to race up the hill to the cheers of the other students. Orla found herself pushed on by those behind her. Then they breasted the hill and once more on the flat they began to spread out. Sally was in front, her long legs spraying out tiny pebbles as she sprinted round a bend.

Orla settled her pace, slowing a little to let Helen Shaw past. She felt a surge of pleasure as she ran, breathing without effort. She was fit, used to running through city streets, the sooner to get home and away from curious eyes. The island road, although bumpy, had more give in it than the streets and by the time they were on the home straight there were only two of them in the race—herself and Sally. Sally was still ahead as the house came into sight but Orla knew now that she could beat her anytime she pleased. She had lots left and she was a fast finisher. As she flew along she wondered when she had felt this happy. The lightness of the air, her strength, the pleasure of competing—I'm normal, she thought.

She was actually beginning to plan her tactics, deciding that she would start to close in in another five yards, when she suddenly thought—what was she doing? Sally, Sally who knew her secret, she couldn't afford to beat Sally. She stumbled. Sally looked back, then continued on, almost there.

Orla set up a miserable jog. She would have preferred to just sit down on the side of the road, but she didn't want to have to start offering explanations to the others when they caught up.

Sally was sitting at the door of the house with a glass of water in her hand. "What happened?"

"I don't know. I just ran out of steam, I suppose."

Sally gave her arm a friendly squeeze. "Bad luck. And you were going so well."

Orla lay on her bed listening to the movement and noise on the landing outside. The *bean an tí* was in the kitchen preparing a picnic for them. She was making potato salad, washing lettuce, hard-boiling eggs. "It would be a sin to eat inside on such a day," she said. As soon as she had the picnic ready they could take it to the *Trá Bán*, have their swim, and eat afterward. That way they would get the whole of the afternoon.

"Look at me," someone shrieked, "I'm so white. How can I get out in a bikini?"

"Never mind that, look at the size of my thighs. And"—the voice rose in outrage—"that can't be cellulite. I cannot have cellulite at seventeen. It's not scientifically possible."

Orla couldn't understand her mood. Usually she felt nothing but contempt for such silliness, but now she had a sudden longing to join in. Perhaps it was the sunshine that was filling her with strange desires. She wanted to go with the others to the beach. She wanted to be silly and loud, seeking attention. She wanted boys to notice her and fancy her and ask her out.

She felt her loneliness acutely. It would always be like this, only getting worse as the years went by. That touch of Sally's hand on her arm had unlocked something inside Orla so that for the first time in years, she admitted that what she wanted, more than anything else, was to be a normal girl.

Angry tears scalded her cheeks. "You can't, you fool," she told herself.

She imagined Sally's expression, her laughter when she saw Orla's wig, tugged off by the force of the waves, floating out to sea. She couldn't go swimming with them, today or any day.

There was a bang on her door; then it opened and eight faces peered in at her. Something had happened to the others too, for normally they would never open her door. Or perhaps they were picking up her own softened attitude.

"Are you ready?"

"Hurry up."

"How can you bear it in here? It's stifling."

She looked at Sally's smirking face, at the others, ready to jump whatever way Sally ordered. And she remembered another, younger Orla, a twelve-year-old girl saying to her parents, "Don't worry, it's just a disease, just an old cancer and I'm going to beat it."

Where had all that courage gone? Where had it come from? Here she was, five years older, and frightened of a few jeers. She, the fighter whom everybody had been so proud of.

Orla jumped onto the floor. "Don't let me keep you," she said, "I can't go swimming."

Her eyes met Sally's, locked on to them.

Sally said, "Your allergy, I suppose?"

She could hear the sneer in her voice.

"Actually, no." And before she had time to think she had reached up and yanked off the wig.

There were gasps, and then silence.

Jane Hogan squeaked out, "My God, you're as bald as a coot."

Orla had dreaded and feared this moment for five years. And now she was laughing! Perhaps it was hysteria, she didn't know, but soon the others had joined in. Then they started firing questions at her: How did it happen, when did it happen, what did it feel like to wear a wig?

"Shut up, the lot of you," Sally roared. "Have you no manners?"

She moved over to stand beside Orla. "You don't have to answer any questions," she said in a gentle voice that nobody had heard before. "It's your own business."

Now that Orla had started, however, she couldn't stop. All the silence and secrecy of those years was being swept away. She felt her rib cage expand as if a weight had been removed from on top of her heart.

She told them everything.

Outside the sun shone brassily. On the kitchen table the picnic lay forgotten. Thoughts of swimming had vanished as they all listened to Orla's story. When she was finished there was another silence. Then Sally said, "I think you're bloody brave, that's what I think. I also think you look great without the wig—no—I'm not just saying it. You've lovely cheekbones and great eyes. You kinda look like Sinéad O'Connor."

There was a chorus of, "Yeah, brilliant. Just like Sinéad."

"But you've got to start wearing more eye makeup,"

Sally went on. "You've got to emphasize those eyes. Kohl, I think and lots of mascara. And I've got some terrific fake tattoos—how about a butterfly on your temple?"

Bossy Sally began to organize everything. Orla didn't mind now; in fact she was delighted.

They ate the picnic at the kitchen table after explaining, with Orla's permission, the whole situation to the *bean an tí*.

"We've no time to go swimming," Sally declared. "We're going to get Orla ready for the *ceilidhe* tonight. And we tell nothing to nobody, right? If anyone asks we act vague and say, 'Yeah, she must have decided to change her image.' It's only Orla has the right to tell her story so keep your mouths shut."

The girls began to rummage through their suitcases, looking for the most flattering outfit for Orla. Finally she was arrayed in Sally's wide silk trousers with a dark blue belly-top of Jane's.

Sally sat her in the window and started painting her face. She wouldn't allow Orla to look until she had finished. Then she handed her a mirror. "What do you think?"

Orla looked. Huge, deep-blue eyes, a soft pink mouth, cheekbones, yes, and a butterfly on her temple. She reached up to caress her skull, realizing for the first time how delicately sculpted it was. Tears prickled behind her eyelids. "I look—"

"You look stunning."

And in utter amazement Orla replied, "I do."

"Just remember," Sally said, "that's a very dramatic look. Don't ever dream of going out without your eye makeup or the whole effect will be ruined. Now, go and look at yourself in the long mirror on the landing. We'll wait for you downstairs."

Orla did as she was bid. At the turn of the stairs she stopped and looked up to where a skylight let in a square of darkening sky.

"Okay, God," she whispered. "We're quits. But enough is enough and the least I expect from You after this is an easy ride."

Then she ran down into the hall to join the others.

ITA DALY

ITA DALY was born in the West of Ireland and moved to Dublin with her family when she was twelve. She has always written and always known that she wanted to be a writer, though she earned her living for eleven years teaching English and Spanish in high school. She has published five novels and one collection of stories for adults and two short novels for children. She lives in Dublin with her husband and daughter and a very neurotic cat.

To Dream of
White Horses

by June Considine

L ast night I watched a nature documentary. I saw
     newborn squid rising from the bed of an ocean
with nothing to protect them from the lurking dan-
gers floating all around them. No mother. No father.
Their parents had paid the ultimate price for their
brief encounter by dying as soon as the eggs were laid.
They left nothing behind except their genetic imprint
and an inherited instinct for survival.

The documentary made me think of Zoe. The miracle baby. An orphan before she was born. Her photograph was on the front pages of newspapers. Her birth
by cesarean operation was reported on the television
evening news. A skid on an icy road and her parents
wiped out before their first child was born. Good me-
dia material. She was still kicking when her mother's

body was rushed to the maternity hospital. Even then, Zoe was a survivor.

We met in February. A cold day, the wind sharp as glass on my face. I huddled into my parka, killing time on a park bench in Stephen's Green. I'd been spending a lot of time in the park, holed up until school was over and I could safely return to the apartment. Sooner or later someone always sat down beside me. Old guys with yellow eyes and booze in paper bags. Old women with memories to spend. Mothers watching their children feeding the ducks. But, on this particular day, even the ducks were sheltering out of sight on the island in the center of the lake.

Zoe was drawing on the pavement near where I was sitting, a kaleidoscope of colored chalk scattered around her. Her concentration was absolute. I could have been invisible, even when I moved from the bench to see what she was doing. She had drawn a city. High buildings, stick people without features, crazily tilted shops, and office blocks dominated by a hulking mountain in the background. Its height seemed to drain the landscape, dimming the brighter street colors until everything appeared to lie in its dreary dark shadows. In the corner of the picture I saw a tear. A solitary shining bubble. When I looked closer, I realized there was a tiny figure curled inside it.

Zoe sighed impatiently, as if I had disturbed her, and glanced up. Her eyes were a greeny gray, like the sea on those overcast days when clouds are low and the rain is hanging in the air. I know about the sea. I used to watch it from my bedroom window when it roared toward the shore, foaming high and thrashing the rocks.

"Shouldn't you be at school instead of hanging around here flirting with hypothermia?" she asked. She began to draw again but the feverish concentration had left her. She stroked the pavement, lightly blurring the shape into the mountain with the flat of her hand.

"I should. But I'm not. End of story."

"Touchy subject?"

"No. Just a boring one. It's more educational to watch you work."

"Then we'll have to postpone your education for another day." She gathered up the chalk and stood stamping pins and needles from her feet. Her black ankle boots were scratched and covered in chalk dust. As I stood staring at her, not sure what move to make, rain began to fall. We took shelter under a tree as a sudden heavy shower swirled over the pavement, chasing the stick people and splashing off the buildings until only the dark head of the mountain remained.

Then it too merged into the running colors and disappeared.

"Your drawing is destroyed," I said, wondering how she could be so calm. Hours of detailed work gone in an instant.

"So what?" She shrugged. "I can do another one tomorrow." She sounded bored. "Now it's time to eat. Like to share some hot chocolate and doughnuts with me?"

"That's the best offer I've had all day."

She allowed me to carry her rucksack to the bench. It looked far too heavy for her slight figure and, like her boots, had seen much wear and tear. We wiped off the rain and sat down. She took out a flask and a bag of doughnuts. Two ducks waddled from behind the foliage on the island. They nose-dived into the freezing water to prove there was a serious shortage of food and we rewarded them with sugary crumbs.

I had seen homeless people sleeping in shop doorways. They sat on O'Connell Bridge and held cardboard placards in front of them. Their hard, searching eyes carried the secrets of an invisible city. Drugs, alcohol, fights, loneliness, the police moving them on, the long winter nights in the open. It was difficult to connect that world with Zoe. Yet she too sought shelter in abandoned houses or slept in the basements of office blocks. She told me that she was thirteen when she went on the road for the first time, escaping from her grandparents, who smothered her with anxiety and rules that had to be instantly obeyed. She was found by the police as she was about to board the ferry at Dun Laoghaire but a year later she ran away again. By the time she was eighteen and in charge of her own life she had run away six times. "Alternative living," she called it. My father would have called it bumming around.

Now she was twenty-five. Her grandparents were dead and the hardness of the city was beginning to touch her mouth. A shadow of things to come but when she laughed and tossed her hair she was beautiful.

Sometimes she was commissioned to paint murals on the walls and hoardings of building sites. Cheerful scenes to hide the destruction going on behind them. Mostly she drew on pavements and hoped that people would throw money at her. She never stayed in the same place for long. When she grew tired of city noises, she headed for the mountains. Every mountain has its ruins, she said, and she would hole up in one of those tumbledown cottages until the streets drew her back again. Her life sounded wild and out of control. I had a sudden urge to walk away from her and half-rose from the bench, ready with excuses. She reached out her hand and gripped my wrist. "I need a squat for a few days. Don't suppose you happen to know of an empty house where no one's looking too closely?"

I didn't want to tell her about Seaview Tower. I didn't want her disturbing the spirits that rested uneasily there. I felt her grip soften as her hand slipped into mine. "A roof . . . that's all I need, Eoin. Even if it's leaking I can put up the tent inside the house."

"I know a place." I pulled her to her feet. "Come on. I'll show you."

We took the bus to Corry Pier. White horses were slanting in on the tide, sweeping away the smell of seaweed and the beached, dead jellyfish. I carried her rucksack across the road toward the embankment I'd always used as a shortcut to the house.

A tall, round tower house guarding the sea. Rosa's house. So flaky and old that only crazy people would want to live in it. My home for fourteen years. So close to the shore that sand seeped under the doors, filling corners and crevices, a gritty trail under our feet. In winter the walls wept and sprouted mushrooms. The stained-glass panes above the front door cracked at the first sign of frost. Such inconveniences, when she noticed them, never bothered Rosa, my mother. She would proudly point to the carvings on the doors and the oak floorboards in the drawing room that had once been part of a great ship, insisting I was lucky to live in a house with such character. When my father sold it to a property developer and we drove away he ordered me not to look back. "The past is a sharp corner," he said. "Once you turn it there's not a lot of sense in looking behind."

"Crazy!" Zoe stood back and gazed at the round walls. She took a chisel and mallet from her rucksack. I hammered and levered loose the planks covering the windows and front door, regretting the impulse that had brought me back here.

"I don't think this is a good idea," I said. "You'll probably be able to find somewhere much better if you look around."

"No. This is it. It's cool."

When I forced open the hall door a newspaper rose from the floor, spreading yellow wings as the wind gusted under it. Zoe kicked aside a beer can, dismissing the litter and the cold and the moldering smells. She didn't notice the ghosts.

"You won't recognize this place when you see it

again," she said, and hummed softly as she unpacked her rucksack.

In the bus on the way to the apartment I imagined her moving through the rooms. She would climb the spiral stairs, the fifth step squeaking in protest when she stepped upon it. Her fingers would touch the gouged wood on the banisters where I had carved my name before leaving with my father. She would stand in my parents' empty bedroom and look down to the wilderness that was once our back garden. Under the weeds and the sucking creepers, there were snowdrops, crocuses, and daffodils. As night drew down, she would climb the attic stairs and stand in the gloom of Rosa's studio. The paints were still there. Rusting brushes in jars of cloudy water. Canvases stacked against the walls. Beyond the window she would watch the lights of Corry Head illuminate the darkness, spilling like a necklace around the lower slopes and climbing upward to the summit, glowing and winking. A golden oasis. Would she feel my mother's presence at her shoulder? Artist to artist. Her breath whispering, "See how the night shines. But it's not real, you know. There's a void beyond the glory and that's what I have to paint." How many times had she breathed those words into my ears? Our eyes fixed on the quivering headland as we tried to imagine the secrets hidden between the folds of light. No . . . Zoe would not hear my mother's whispering voice. She was a survivor. Seaview Tower would be her shelter until she was ready to move on, nothing more.

In the apartment I saw the bottle of whiskey on the coffee table. A bad sign; my father usually waited until the evening meal was over before pouring his first drink.

"You took your time today," he said when I entered the kitchen. He always made the same comment when I was late, but I'd never heard him ask the reason.

"Smells good." I sniffed appreciatively when he opened the oven door and carried a casserole dish to the table.

"How was school?"

"Oh, you know . . . same as usual."

We began to eat. The silence was a sullen space between us. Sometimes I imagined having witty, stimulating conversations with him. But we never managed more than a few sentences before the effort of communicating exhausted us. When he sold Seaview Tower he gave the furniture away. Two men from the St. Vincent de Paul Society came and removed everything except my mother's paintings. I believed he was going to bring them to the apartment.

"No space," he said when the time came to leave. He allowed me to choose one painting, then firmly closed the door of her studio.

The painting hung in my bedroom, a feathery image of green, almost a whisper on canvas as it drifted above the strong burgeoning roots that thrust downward, forcing their way between rocks and the seething underground world of insect and animal. I was eight years old when she painted it and had been repelled by the images. "It's awful—ugly! . . . Trees aren't like that at all. You're always making everything look different."

"Ah, but think, Eoin." She always smiled when she explained things to me. "Without roots we have no trees. Can you imagine such a dead world? It's not only what we see and touch and understand that matters. The things we cannot see or touch or understand are just as important."

My father used to wink when he heard her talking like that. "It beats me what's going on in your mother's crazy, wonderful head." He'd press his lips against her forehead. A time came when he stopped calling her crazy. It became a loaded word. He described her paintings as Rosa's therapy. I can still remember the expression on her face when he said that. As if she had felt the sting of a small stone on her skin.

The property developer who bought Seaview Tower planned to build luxury apartments with balconies and glass elevators and a view. The sea shimmering in sunshine. Corry Head shimmering at dusk.

"Don't go back there," warned my father. "There'll be heavy machinery. I don't want you getting in the way of the builders."

Months later, when I did return, the house was still standing. The panes above the front door were smashed and graffiti had been sprayed over the outside walls. Cider cans, hamburger cartons, and used condoms littered the hall. Thieves had taken the wrought-iron gates. My house had become a sick joke, a hulk. I longed for a crane with a hanging ball to smash it to pieces. But the property developer was having trouble with planning permission. His apartments with a view were still on hold. Soon afterward, he had the doors and windows boarded up.

My father bought modern furniture for our new life. Streamlined, minimalist, said the saleswoman. Perfect for an apartment. A fold-up table, spring-back beds, built-in closets. A space for everything. He used one of the rooms as his office. His business card read BILL CARTER. FINANCIAL CONSULTANT.

"Working from home is the way of the future," he said.

I figured it was because he couldn't cut the morning traffic with a hangover. Before Rosa left us he used to travel all the time. New York, Boston, Sydney, Tokyo. He was always landing or taking off on planes. He brought me presents from abroad, denim jackets with American designer labels, the latest computer games, books on astronomy. He bought my mother perfume at airports and was furious when she began to throw the unopened bottles into the garbage.

We never had to talk in those days. Rosa was the conduit between us. She told me he was proud and delighted when I earned good grades, made the school athletic squad, joined the debating society. I believed in this dream figure she created and then discovered she'd left me face to face with a stranger.

He switched on the television. We watched the news and a game show. He sipped whiskey and stared into his glass.

"It's two years today." His voice was flat. "I wondered if you remembered."

"Why should I forget?"

"Are you all right . . . everything okay?"

"Sure. It's just . . . two years. It seems so long when you say it but it's not . . . is it?"

"Time passes, Eoin."

"But it doesn't heal." I wanted to shout at him but that would be real conversation so I said the words to myself and switched television channels. He made no effort to make further conversation. That was fine by me. Talking was disastrous when he was drinking. He'd start by reminiscing about his young days and how hard he'd had to work to achieve his success. Young people didn't know the meaning of hard work because everything was laid on for them. We were the wimp generation, hooked on having a good time at any cost.

"Spoiled from birth . . . that's what you are. You haven't a clue. Nancy boys, all of you." He'd thump my arm, laughing. Big joke. It's a sore spot, just above the elbow. His fist was a hard ball digging deep. I'd hit back hard and he'd hit harder and then it wasn't a game anymore but one of those stag things with the antlers rattling, both of us determined to win. I'd feel sick, unable to stop yet afraid he'd freak out and let his thoughts spill over . . . and then what would we say to each other?

The dream came again that night. White horses, a herd of them rising from the sea, pounding toward me. Their hooves drummed in my ears. I tried to move out of their way but my feet sank in sand. Then they were underneath me and I was rolling over their backs, trying to hold their flailing manes. I went under, sinking deeper and deeper into a void where there was nothing, only the dark silence of drowning. I always woke up on a scream. But there was no scream when I forced my eyes open. Just a grinding moan of relief.

My file was open on the school principal's desk when I entered her office the following morning. Notes forged with my father's signature were stacked beside it. "I must say, Eoin, you look remarkably healthy for someone who's been afflicted by so many ailments." Mrs. Parkinson glanced down at the note on top of the pile. "Your father must be quite worried about you."

"The doctor says my immune system is low. I'll be fine when it builds up again."

"How long will this buildup process take?" She made no effort to hide her sarcasm.

"Soon. I'm on multivitamins and iron tablets."

"Spare me the medical report, Eoin Carter." She handed me a letter. "Give this to your father. I want to see him in here with you on the Monday following midterm break. Then we'll discuss your immune system, among other things. . . . Is that understood?"

Across the bay Corry Head was beginning to glimmer as evening traffic twisted along the steep, narrow roads. Zoe had lit a fire in the old house and driftwood blazed up the chimney. Burning candles jutted from wine bottles. In the flickering flames she seemed to belong to the shadows that had captured the room. She was kneeling on the floor, drawing on the boards, so absorbed I had to call twice before she heard me.

"I found photographs of you in that attic room," she said. "You never told me you used to live here."

"It's a long time ago." I hunched down to examine her drawing. She had just started to work on it. White lines curling like a question mark into empty space.

"Interesting. What's it supposed to mean?"

"Whatever you want it to mean. Who owns the paintings upstairs?"

"My mother. The attic was her studio."

"Cool spot. The light is brilliant . . . not to mention the view. Does she still paint?"

"No. . . . Where did you find the photographs?"

"Stuck in a press with her sketch pads. I'll get them for you."

In the grate the wood burned to fine gray ash. A gas ring fluttered underneath a saucepan, chicken simmering in spices and rice. Familiar smells. I thought about the dinner parties Rosa used to hold. The laughter floating upward into my bedroom. When people stopped coming there were no more spice smells. Some days she did not get out of bed until I came home from school. Then I made sandwiches and we ate them in the kitchen. She would stare at the wall behind me. When I pushed her hair back from her face she winced as if the sun hurt her eyes. But I don't remember any sunshine. Just clouds moving slow over the sea.

"What's depression?" I asked my father.

"It's all about the power of the mind," he said. "The only thing that will make it go away is your own determination." He ran his hand over the window ledge and frowned at the smudge on his fingers.

When Rosa was happy our house was filled with music. I could never imagine the silences returning. The light in her studio burned through the night.

One summer she painted Corry Head. The gorse blazed like a fireball. Purple heather covered the rocks. She painted it with the mist falling down and hiding all the color. I wondered if that was what her life was like. Always trying to escape from behind the mist.

I stared at the photographs that charted our fourteen years together. In one of them I stood between my parents, toothy grin, my hair neatly parted to one side. "Happy families." Zoe grinned. "That's kind of cute."

"Cute?" I placed the album on the mantelpiece, no longer interested. "That's not the word I'd use."

My father was right. The past was a sharp corner. No time to dillydally on the bend.

Every day during midterm break I returned to Seaview Tower, terrified that the builders would have chased her away. The property developer had sorted out his planning problems. Work would begin soon. I imagined throwing myself in front of bulldozers or chaining myself to the front door. Instead, I gathered driftwood and shopped for food in Corrystown. Zoe picked forsythia and placed it in jars on the window ledges. Her drawing on the floor remained unfinished but she used my mother's paints to cover the walls with murals. A circus ring, children and clowns turning somersaults. Her rucksack rested near the front door. A house on a frame. So many pockets and loops, each with a purpose, a storage space, a hanging space. Within a few minutes she could pack everything she needed to exist and carry it on her back.

We were walking along the strand one morning when she told me about the accident. The birth of a miracle baby.

"My mother wanted to see the mountains in snow," she explained. "There were road warnings being broadcast. Is your journey really necessary, that kind of stuff. Why on earth did he have to listen to her? Why?"

I was startled by her anger. It came so fast, as if her breath had suddenly exploded free. Then she tossed her head. "Oh well, what does it matter now?" A question asked in the same dismissive tone she had used when she watched her chalk city float from the pavement.

"Is that why you're always running?" I asked.

"I don't know how to explain." She hesitated for an instant. "No one understands."

"I want to understand. Tell me."

"I'm searching for something I lost before I was born."

"Your parents?"

"No. I've never had to search for them." She held out her long fingers and examined them. "I have my father's fingers. Piano fingers. My mother's eyes. When I smile I look exactly like her. That's what my grandparents always said. My father's family too. They never saw me, just the reflections of their lost children." Her voice was low, a talking to herself sort of voice. "I've always wanted to take them for granted . . . but the dead don't allow it. They leave too many questions behind. My parents were just ordinary people but what happened to them made them extraordinary and they're here . . . all the time in my head. . . ."

I remembered the crush of people in her drawing. The mountain so dark and dominating. The tiny bubble figure.

"Aren't you scared being homeless and on your own all the time?" I asked.

"Does a home stop you from being scared?" She stopped and turned to face me.

"I'm not scared. What makes you think that?"

"Do you want to tell me what's wrong?"

"There's nothing wrong. . . . Everything's cool."

We continued walking by the edge of the shore, adding our footprints to the tiny bird claws and the deep hollows left by the horses from the riding school that had cantered past us. Sand blew in the wind, stinging like needles. We headed toward the beach shelter and sat together on the bench. Zoe used a tissue to remove grit from my eyes. One story borrows another and so I told her about Rosa. The first time I had mentioned her name since she went away.

"Does your father know you come back to the house?" she asked when I fell silent.

"He'd freak if he found out."

"Do the two of you ever talk about her?"

"Never."

"What would happen if you did?"

"He'd blame me . . . I see it in his face all the time."

"What if it's his own guilt you see? His own demons?"

"He doesn't have any. He says he did everything for her and she flung it all back at him."

The beach shelter was still the same. Gray pebble-dash walls with graffiti. The seeping smell of urine. I wondered if the gang still gathered there at night. Brian O'Neill played guitar with a rock band. Morgan Dunne's father was a doctor with a clinic full of pills. One night when Rosa was sleeping I sneaked out and joined them. We played music on ghetto blasters and smoked. We talked about girls and sex and football until Morgan Dunne produced a bottle of vodka. We mixed it with the pills. The sea rolled away from us and the stars streaked across the sky. Blue lights flashed. We were too stupefied to move until the squad car screeched to a halt and the cops came running. They chased us along the hard sand. One of them grabbed me in a rugby tackle.

"That's it, you little scumbag." He breathed hard into the back of my neck. "That's the end of your little game."

Rosa collected me from the Garda station. She rang my father in San Francisco and he arrived home two days early.

"See what you've done to your mother?" He shouted and lifted his fists in the air. I'd never seen him in such a temper. "I hope you're satisfied. You were supposed to look after her when I was away but all you've done is add to her problems." I was beaten for the first time in my life. "Let that be a lesson to you." His hands shook as he placed them on my shoulders. "I don't ever want to do that to you again . . . but I will if it's necessary."

My dreams changed to drowning of another kind. Drowning in Zoe's arms. I wanted to stay there forever, stroking her, kissing her. My tongue moving over her breasts until she moaned and called out my name. Such a wild cry. I woke on the sound, my body releasing its pleasure on the sheets; the spent energy of a fantasy. My skin was on fire. It seemed such an invasion, the things I had done to her without her knowledge. In the bathroom I lit a match and burned the letter from Mrs. Parkinson. Midterm break was over. I flushed the ash down the toilet bowl.

On Monday afternoon two men arrived with tripods and stood at the foot of the embankment.

"I'll have to move on soon." Zoe glanced down at them. "It looks like the action is about to begin."

"I'm going with you," I said. "I've been thinking of nothing else for days."

"That's crazy, Eoin. You're just a boy."

"I'm sixteen. And I'm in love with you."

"Love!" She dismissed the word. "No one has ever loved me."

"Your grandparents did."

"It was never love. Just duty."

"So . . . What do you call my love? Infatuation? A mother fixation? An escape route?"

"Stop it, Eoin." She held her palm toward me, warding off my words. "I don't want to hurt you."

"Let me go with you, Zoe. I won't make demands or anything. I just want to be with you."

She gently pushed me away when I tried to put my arms around her. "There's too many people in my life already, Eoin."

"Dead people," I said. "You don't need them. You've never needed them. You're the most complete person I've ever known."

"I'm always running but I'm still in the same place. Is that what you want?" She touched my forehead with her lips. No passion. Just understanding, so much understanding. "Have the courage to set her free."

They came the following morning. Two diggers churned the front garden. The noise from the engines was overwhelming. A crane was already in position in front of the house. Men in yellow jackets and helmets stood beside it. I ran toward them, shouting. "Stop! There's someone living in there."

"Stand back, lad. There's no one in there." The foreman held out his hands in front of me. I shoved him aside and ran through the open door. Dead embers, burned-out candles. Her rucksack gone.

She had finished the drawing on the floor. In the sunshine spilling through the window the flowing lines were so sharply defined that for an instant they seemed to rise from the floorboards. White horses whirling and circling, onward, outward. An eternal journey of light and shade. Along one wall she had placed my mother's canvases.

"Are you happy now?" The foreman stood in front of me. "I told you the place was empty."

"You drove her away." My fingers locked so hard together they hurt.

"Drove who away? Talk sense, lad. The house was empty when we arrived. Off you go now and let the men get on with their work."

I picked up the first canvas. "I'm taking these paintings with me. They're mine."

He glanced at his watch and sighed impatiently. "Take whatever you want and be fast about it or you'll feel the toe of my boot up your arse."

In the city I searched for Zoe. No chalk marks on the pavement. The buskers on Grafton Street didn't know anyone answering her description. An old woman with a shopping trolley sat on the park bench and threw bread at the ducks. I asked the same question and she shook her head. It was late when I returned home.

"You took your time today." My father lifted steaks

from the grill and laid them on warmed plates. "What kept you?"

"I stayed back at school to work on a French project."

"I see." His tone was even as he began to eat. After a few minutes he laid down his knife and fork and stared at me. His eyes were clear, sparking with anger. "I received an interesting phone call today from Mrs. Parkinson. Remember her? She was wondering why neither of us turned up for a certain meeting she arranged yesterday. Apparently, you were supposed to give me a letter."

"I don't remember any letter."

He ignored my reply. "She also wanted to know why you've been missing so much school lately. But first things first. We'll start with the letter. Show it to me. Immediately!"

"I burned it. . . . I didn't want to worry you."

"That's very kind of you, Eoin. At least it would be if I thought you were telling me the truth. The only thing wrong with your immune system is that it's keeping you alive. What have you been doing when you were not at school . . . huh? Messing around with drugs? Shoplifting? Joyriding? Tell the truth for a change."

"It's none of your business what I do." I was on my

feet, shouting into his face. Not caring anymore. "They knocked it down today. Every brick. It's all gone. Are you happy now that nothing's left?"

"I told you not to go there." He smashed his fist off the table and rose to face me. "But when did you ever do anything you were supposed to do?"

"How would you know? You're never sober long enough to notice."

"How dare you—how dare you." He hit me, his fist slamming against my chest and shoulders. No games this time. I preferred it this way.

"I'm sick of it—do you hear me?" I couldn't stop shouting. "I'm sick of your drinking and your silence and the way you look at me . . . as if I'm to blame. I don't want to go on feeling like this . . . every day feeling I don't deserve to be alive. I want her back again. Do you hear me? I want her back!"

He grabbed me again, holding me hard against his chest until I fell silent. I felt his heart thumping but then I thought . . . maybe it's mine . . . maybe it's both of us. I ran to my room and returned with one of the canvases. He was slumped in a chair, his face in his hands.

"You want to know what I did today?" I asked, my voice quiet now. I placed the canvas in front of him. "I took back our past."

He touched the canvas, his fingers tensed as if they would burn on contact. "I'm so angry, Eoin," he whispered. "Christ! I'm so angry since she went. . . ." I left him staring at her painting. Corry Head with the mist falling.

My mother was placing daffodils in a glass vase the last time I saw her. The morning news was on the radio. Northern Ireland peace process talks. She switched channels and swayed to the music. Our kitchen was filled with white light. I knew her happiness was as transient as the sunshine. I wanted no part of it.

"Hurry home from school, Eoin." She called after me and waved in the direction of the headland. "I want to paint it again. But different this time. Come with me, won't you?"

I nodded and slung my school backpack over my shoulder. I can't remember if I kissed her. I think not. But I hope I did.

After school I went into Dublin city with Morgan Dunne. We played computer games and went to the cinema. It was dark when we reached the beach shelter. Morgan had white pills. We mixed them with cider. I lost time that night. I saw shapes on the sea. A ship with lights sailing over the sand. A circling moon.

As soon as I entered the house I knew it was empty. Yet I searched every room, calling her name over and over again. Then I ran down the embankment and onto the strand. A man walking his dog had seen a woman on the rocks below Corry Head. He worried because the waves were high. A spring tide, treacherous.

I rang the police and then my father in New York. I've no memory of how we passed the time while we waited for news of her return. People called and spoke in quiet voices. Their fixed, reassuring smiles terrified me. The search lasted for three days until her body was swept ashore on an incoming tide.

The call of cormorants rose from the rocks. A shrill warning as I climbed through the barrier at the end of Corry Pier. I stood on the narrow ledge staring down into the water. Zoe had shaped my nightmare on the floorboards. White horses riding the night. Beneath the turmoil I sensed the stillness, the invisible depths of silence. I imagined my body falling like a stone, drawn down under the waves until it was floating in the timeless rhythm of tides. My heart began to beat faster. A step closer and it would be over. I swayed forward. How could she leave me with nothing but guilt to mark our years together?

Spray stung my eyes. I couldn't remember the last time I cried. My anger flowed into the sea. White horses lifted it, tossed it high, and gave it back to me, a spent force. For a dizzy instant my mother and Zoe merged and became one, moving away from me as the tide raged upward against the pier. Pictures I could not see or touch or understand flowed around me. They formed a space that I must not be afraid to enter. A space where pain had to be endured so that it could pass away. Where the waves wasted upon the sands before turning to gather strength for a new day.

The moon came out. A pale lantern shining. A room blazing with the light of many candles. I imagined Zoe trudging over mountains. Alone in an empty landscape, thinking thoughts of what might have been. My mother came slowly from the mist where I had walked since she died.

"Rosa . . . Rosa." I whispered her name. "What happened to you? That's the most awful part . . . not knowing."

No one answered. No one ever would. Some questions have no answers. White horses reared toward us, ready to carry her safely home.

Headlights swept the sea. A car braked sharply. A door slammed.

"Eoin!" My father's voice carried above the waves. It could have been a question. Or maybe it was a cry. I heard his footsteps on the pier. I turned and hurried toward the sound.

JUNE CONSIDINE

JUNE CONSIDINE was born in Dublin. Her twelve books for children and young adults include the popular Luvender fantasy series and the Beachwood series for young teenagers. Her young adult novel *View from a Blind Bridge* was short-listed for the Bisto Book of the Year Award 1992–1993. She has also published short stories for adults and has just completed her first adult novel. She and her husband have a son and two daughters. She lives in the coastal village of Malahide, near Dublin, with her family, and works as a journalist and magazine editor.

GOOD GIRL

by Marita Conlon-McKenna

hrissy yelled.

C She yelled so hard that the concrete walls and the sand, cement, and stone seemed to shudder, the sound ricocheting along the red tin roof . . . still no one heard.

"What you doing, Chrissy?" inquired her little sister, Gemma.

Chrissy ignored her and kept on brushing her long auburn hair till it shone, falling thick and glossy down her back.

Gemma watched her in the bedroom mirror, her eyes filled with idle curiosity.

"Are you going to put a band on, or tie some of it up?"

"No." She smiled. Ian liked her hair long and loose.

"Are you going on a date?" pleaded Gemma. "Is that it!"

Chrissy widened her eyes, trying not to give much away as her sister bounced on the corner of the bed.

"Curiosity killed the cat," she muttered in exasperation. Why were little sisters such brats! Gemma spent half her time watching and copying her, sneaking her jewelry and CDs, and now the latest thing was her perfume and nail polish. Once Gemma got a bit taller, it would probably be Chrissy's clothes.

"Have you nothing better to do Gemma, honestly!"

Gemma looked contrite for about two seconds.

"Nope!" she declared. "You know, when I grow up, Chrissy, I'm going to be just like you!"

Their eyes met. Chrissy smiled. "Well, Gemma! Do I look all right? What d'ya think?"

Gemma wrapped her arms around her shoulders. "You look drop-dead gorgeous!"

"Hey, Gemma, be a pet and see if my shoes are under the bed."

Gemma scrabbled around till she pulled out the tan suede lace-ups.

"There you go!" she said.

Chrissy pulled her denim jacket off the back of the chair, tucking her white shirt into her new jeans. It had taken a month's baby-sitting money to buy them, but now, seeing how well they fit, it was worth it.

Just as she was about to leave, her older sister, Anna, looked in the door. "You going out again, Chrissy!"

She nodded.

"Got all your homework done?"

"Aye!" she replied through gritted teeth.

"Where are you meeting him?"

"Up the town."

"Be careful, Chrissy!" Anna looked concerned. "You know what folk in this place are like!"

Chrissy shrugged. Anna was such an old fogey. She was only nineteen, but she might as well be forty-nine, judging by the way she went on. She was studying at Queens University, history and politics, and was still dating Ray, her childhood sweetheart. The two of them were so boring! All they ever talked about was saving to get married. Anna spent her time studying or else sitting downstairs with Mam and Dad and Ray watching the television. Catch Chrissy being like that!

"By the way, Anna, his name's Ian and he's not a monster!"

"I know!" said Anna, smiling. "Just be careful. Politicians signing peace agreements and the IRA and the Loyalists talking about cease-fires and handing in their weapons doesn't mean that things are safe and settled here in the North yet."

Chrissy stood waiting outside the shop window of Wellworth's. Funny, it wasn't like Ian to be late. He was usually dead punctual. She glanced at her watch; there was bound to be some good reason. She smiled, her eyes searching the distant street for his tall loping figure and floppy hair. She loved the way he walked and talked and was so polite and mannerly, even taking her hand when they crossed the road. He was better-looking than all the boys she knew, much taller and with clear skin, and blue eyes that almost took her breath away. He always smelled of expensive after-shave and wore nice clothes, not just the sweat pants and football shirts like the rest of the lads she knew wore. He didn't shout or swear at people he passed in the street—he wasn't like that; Ian was different!

It was four months since they'd met. Imagine meeting at a school debate; it sounded so corny, the boys in their black blazers and the girls in their knitted green sweaters and tartan skirts.

The motion had been defeated, and afterward she had got chatted up by the handsome team captain. The debate had been organized as part of the Program for Mutual Understanding, bringing the pupils of the local Catholic school and the Protestant grammar school together. There had been plenty of mutual understanding, all right, that night under the watchful gaze of Sister Patricia and the rest of the teachers as the students mingled. Ian and herself fell into conversation about their closing arguments, he telling her that he wanted to study law like his father.

"Hey, Chrissy!"

She almost jumped with fright. It was Eilish Dunne. Eilish was a year ahead of her in school. Petite with peroxide-blond hair.

"You got a light, Chrissy?"

Chrissy shook her head. She didn't smoke.

" 'Tis a nice evening," murmured the other girl. Chrissy tried to be polite, but to tell the truth she didn't much like Eilish and her cronies. Eilish had a chip on her shoulder and blamed everyone for the fact that her father was serving a prison sentence. The fact that he'd been caught making petrol bombs in a shed at the bottom of their garden didn't seem to matter. Eilish and a few other girls were always getting into trouble at school and gave some of the nuns a terrible time.

"My friends and I are going down by the lakeshore for a bit of a walk, d'ya want to come?"

"No thanks, I'm waiting for someone," Chrissy said. "Your fellah is it?"

It was none of the other girl's business. Chrissy wished she'd shove off and leave her alone.

"He's a nice-looking lad!" said Eilish, smirking. Chrissy stared at her. "Saw him, so I did, not more than half an hour ago, down by the lake. Looking for you, so he was."

Chrissy hesitated.

"We're going back down that way," cajoled Eilish. "We may as well all go together."

As if from nowhere three more girls appeared, Teresa Brogan and Eilish linking arms with her as if they were best friends, as they passed down along the high street.

'Twas a good walk, but at least it was a lovely evening, and Ian would be there waiting for her. The others chatted among themselves, almost ignoring her, as they crossed over the bridge and the winding pathway that led to the small lake. With relief she spotted the tall blowing rushes and reeds and heard the *slip-slap* of the water against the shore. Two or three small wooden rowboats were moored in the distance. Ian had promised to take her rowing when the weather got better.

"Where is he? I don't see him," she said, suddenly anxious.

"He's around somewhere," murmured Teresa.

"Down there!" declared Eilish. "Beside the old boat-house."

Chrissy couldn't see him.

"Look inside!"

She felt the palms of their hands against her back and the dull thud of the door closing behind her.

"Chrissy! D'ya hear me!"

Chrissy nodded. Her eyes were sore from crying, her throat sore from yelling. Someone had a light; it made her blink.

"What are ye doing, wasting your time on a fellah like him! You should have more sense. Our own lads not good enough, is it!"

"You're part of a community, youse can't go letting us down hanging round with the likes of him. We don't take kindly to it!"

She winced in pain as the metal tip of a boot caught her on the shins.

"You're not listening to me!" hissed one of the older girls. "We're only trying to help you, give you a bit of good advice."

She sat dumb, not willing to enrage them.

"Did you ever meet his daddy?" questioned Teresa. "He's a right grand man, involved in the Orange Order, a leading member of the Lodge. All them Protestants stick together. You should see him marching with the rest of them through the town on the Twelfth of July with their bowler hats and sashes and them banners of King Billy, beating their drums as if they owned the place and could drive us Catholics away!"

"I never met him," Chrissy said softly. Ian had told her about his family, his father and mother and brother and sister, and yet had made no mention of bringing her home to meet any of them. The two of them usually just met up the town or at the cinema or somewhere down around here.

"Like father, like son!" hissed Eilish.

"His daddy put my brother away for four years, so he did!" jeered Teresa.

"He made sure they gave Eilish's dad more than ten years!" added Brenda.

Chrissy's blood ran cold. One of the girls lit a cigarette. Chrissy watched as she blew a ring of smoke in her face.

"We don't want to hurt you, Chrissy," said Brenda in a smarmy voice. "We're only trying to help you, warn you. You're from a good family, a nice mum and dad, and that kid sister of yours and that brain-box sister, the one that goes to college. You must all be very proud!"

Fingers of fear ran up her spine. They knew so much about her family . . . too much!

"Chrissy girl! You got to learn that there are things a good Catholic girl should do and not do!"

She bit her lip.

"Will you be a good girl?" asked the older girl earnestly, her dark eyes and narrow acne-marked face staring at Chrissy.

"I am a good girl," she whispered softly. "Ian and I are just good friends, we see each other . . ."

"Well, I'm right glad to hear it," replied the dark one seriously. "Ah, but you shouldn't have mentioned his name. It upsets me thinking about the likes of him. I told you to forget him!"

Brenda passed her the cigarette.

Pain seared through Chrissy's hand as the cigarette was shoved against her skin. She could smell it burning her, sticking to her almost. Oh God! She was going to be sick.

Within seconds they did it again so it felt like her two hands and wrists were on fire.

"You know something, Chrissy, you're a pretty girl."

She could sense them all standing close beside her, blowing smoke in her eyes, considering. She tightened up, waiting for the pain. Relief flooded through her as the girls finished their cigarettes and stubbed them out on the floor.

"She's learnt her lesson!" coughed the leader, turning and walking away from her.

They must be going to let her go.

Some of them had left. It must be dark outside by now. They'd have to let her go real soon. Her mam would have a search party out looking for her. The windows of the boathouse were too small for her to climb through, and there was no likelihood of anyone even walking down this way until early morning. She sat in the gathering darkness.

Eilish was back, standing beside her.

"Eilish!" whispered Chrissy. "Help me!"

Eilish stared at her coldly.

"You've got to help, please!"

Eilish marched off, leaving Teresa to guard her.

Eilish returned carrying a rusty pair of shears.

"Look what I found!" she said, grinning.

Chrissy tried to control the sob of fear that threatened to overwhelm her.

They were going to tar and feather her, kneecap her—memories of newspaper headlines flooded her brain.

"Nice pair of jeans she's got!" whined Teresa, touching the denim.

"Nice and new, I'd say," said Eilish.

"Let me!" Teresa grabbed the shears.

Chrissy tensed as the cold steel pressed against her leg, cutting the blue denim in a long gaping line. The shears cut and cut, nipping her legs, both Teresa and Eilish laughing uproariously as the jeans peeled back.

"Now I think she needs a haircut, Teresa. That long hair has gone right out of fashion!"

They both giggled.

Eilish grabbed at the shears.

Chrissy watched as the long curves of her hair fell on the floor, onto her lap. Already her head felt lighter.

Eilish stopped cutting it at chin level.

"Here, give us a go!" pleaded her friend. "I'll cut it the way you've got yours. Pity we didn't bring a bottle of bleach with us."

They were going to scalp her.

Chrissy tensed as the blades moved across her beneath her hair.

" 'Tis all uneven," jeered Eilish. "Wonder what her

boyfriend will think of that!" Then the clipping stopped.

Automatically Chrissy put her hands to her head, touching the spiky tufts of hair that covered her skull. How could it be that only a few hours ago she'd been sitting in her bedroom safe, brushing her hair?

"Can't have traitors! Can't have betrayers!" They knew that in her mind she was trying to escape them, using her thoughts to protect herself.

"Isn't that a pretty white top!" murmured Eilish. "Bet your mammy ironed and washed that for you?"

Chrissy stared ahead, counting the number of blocks in the wall.

"Well, we'd better give her something to really try and wash!"

She gasped as they tore her shirt open and stroked the blade against her skin, nicking it slightly, the blood seeping slowly, to stain the white shirt pink.

Dr. Grogan had left over an hour ago. He'd given her a tetanus injection and something for the pain and to relax her. He'd put sterile gauze on her gashes and stitched the cut on her leg. Her two sore hands lay dressed and bandaged on top of her gingham duvet.

Her mam and dad suddenly looked old and scared,

both afraid to leave her. She couldn't help it, but she just wasn't able to stop shaking. It was Anna and Ray who'd found her, crying and frightened, trying to find her way home. There was no question of the police being involved. This was a night they all wanted to forget.

Gemma passed her the sunflower-patterned writing paper and pen. Bending her fingers hurt, but it was only a short note that she wanted to write. Gemma waited while she sealed the envelope.

"Do you want another drink or slice of toast or anything before I go to school?"

Chrissy shook her head.

Her sister had been waiting on her hand and foot since it happened. Gemma had cried for over an hour the first morning that she saw her, and had got so angry and upset that Mam had to give her a day off school to calm down.

"Now promise, Gemma! You'll be there on time. Don't let me down!" Chrissy said.

"I promise, Chrissy, I'll go straight from school."

Chrissy watched as her sister shoved the yellow envelope into her school bag.

All day Chrissy waited.

It was near teatime when Gemma got home.

"Gemma!" Chrissy called.

Gemma stood at the bottom of the bed. She looked tired.

"Well, did you meet him?" Chrissy asked. "Did you catch him on his way home?"

Gemma looked crestfallen. She bent down and began to unzip her school bag, taking out the envelope.

"Ah, Gemma! You promised me you'd go!" shouted Chrissy. "Don't tell me that you forgot about it!"

Gemma was hesitant. "I did go, Chrissy! I had to wait for ages. They had a late physics class or something. He was coming out with four other boys and I stopped him and gave him your letter."

"Did he read it! Did he open it!"

Gemma narrowed her eyes.

"He gave it back to me. You'd think I was just some little kid that he didn't know. He just handed it straight back to me."

"Did he say anything?" whispered Chrissy, her stiffened fingers twisting the buttons on her pajamas.

"He said that he was very tied up with his studies at the moment and to give you his kind regards!"

Chrissy moaned, an unnatural sound that came from deep within her, where the hurt was.

"That's when he gave me back your letter." Gemma rushed to the bedside, shoving in beside Chrissy, thumping the pillow fiercely. "I told him! I told him . . . I said you're a stupid proddy git! All his friends heard me."

"What did he . . . what did he say?" sighed Chrissy.

"They laughed. They all laughed, they made jeer of me. I told him that I was only saying what you'd put in the letter, that I felt just like you, I hated him!"

Chrissy lay back against the pillows, silent, considering.

Gemma watched her. Her sister's frizzy ginger hair a mess, her green eyes puzzled, almost afraid, waiting.

Chrissy took a deep breath, pulling it right up through her.

"Good girl," she whispered.

MARITA CONLON-MCKENNA

MARITA CONLON-MCKENNA is the author of the best-selling trilogy, *Children of the Famine,* which includes *Under the Hawthorn Tree* which has been translated into many languages. Among other prizes, it won the International Reading Association Award (Fiction, Older Readers Category) in the United States. She has also won the Bisto Book of the Year Award and the Reading Association of Ireland Award. Her most recent books include, for young readers, *Fields of Home* and *In Deep Dark Wood,* and, for adults, *The Magdalen* and *Promised Land.* She lives in Dublin with her family.

LANDLOCKED

by Helena Mulkerns

Outside Benny's roadhouse, the tall, rotating sign blinked red and yellow, beckoning diners in off the West Texas highway. Kate jumped off the bus at the edge of the car park and scurried under it into the restaurant. It was already ten minutes to eleven, just enough time to get ready for the night shift.

In the staff bathroom, she quickly changed into her brown polyester waitress uniform and flat shoes. Almost the worst thing about this job was having to submit to brown polyester and flat shoes. And the badge with her name on it so that perfect strangers could address her with the familiarity normally reserved for the family dog. Kate walked out into the staff area, where another waitress, Ai Liên, was at the table inspecting a packet of photographs.

The manager paired Kate and Ai Liên off together frequently for the night shift. Mysterious aliens with bizarre accents as opposed to the more familiar Mexican ones, they were the odd couple on the roster. This was what broke the ice between them, although they were from different ends of the planet. Since nobody could pronounce Kate's real name, Catríona, they called her C.J.—for Catríona Jane—which nobody had ever called her in her life. Ai Liên's name got Texanized as Eileen, which intrigued Kate, who had never met a Vietnamese girl before, let alone one called Eileen.

"Have fun with Chatterbox Charlie!" sputtered Lori, the waitress from the early shift, as Ai Liên bustled silently out into the restaurant.

"I will."

Everybody thought Ai Liên was unfriendly, because she was so quiet, but Kate just found her a little reserved, perhaps a little more in control of herself than the others. It was an attribute she found intriguing.

Outside, the restaurant clock ticked five past eleven. The clock ticked and the Formica gleamed. Along every highway in every state, every Benny's was streamlined to please. Smooth synthetic surfaces and plastic plaid-covered seats. Fans circulated overhead, and bleak round ceiling lights twinkled down like illuminated tranquilizers. The piped music added a clean, happy touch.

You'll be proud to be on the Benny's Family Team, the training video said. *A clean, happy work environment that's a home away from home.*

She'd only wound up there by accident. Her parents had let her come to America because Shay, her *so-called* boyfriend, was going to take good care of her throughout. It was really the luckiest chance for her, to spend the summer away, on the J-1 visa, which allowed Irish students to spend summer months working in America, before going home in October, in time for college. It hadn't been easy persuading her parents.

"When I was young, if you went to America, you stayed there. That's why there's so many Irish Americans," Dad had said.

"But the world is smaller now, though," said Kate. "This way—I get to see America and come back again."

"Well, I suppose I'd have to admit there are days when I wake up and wonder what would have happened if I'd gone myself," her mother told her, somewhat mysteriously.

There had been days lately when Kate had been sorry she'd ever left Ireland. Things hadn't worked out as planned. She'd wanted so much to see America, and for Shay and herself to have a good time. They'd planned to work for two months in Boston, then do the Great American Road Trip, driving all across to San Francisco along the old Route 66, like the song.

But Shay had changed when he got to Boston. He worked in his uncle's bar until all hours of the night, while she waitressed during the day shift in a busy restaurant downtown and hardly saw him. It was like they were in separate time zones. He might wake her up when he came in, and sometimes he would be all messed up and tell her he missed her. Other times he just fell into bed, not bothering with conversation.

One night in early August, when he didn't come home at all, Kate sat up until dawn in the dark kitchen, eating buttered toast and drinking the last of the Barry's tea they'd brought from Dublin. The hours went by, ticking painstakingly away on the greasy old kitchen clock, left by some long-forgotten tenant. Three o'clock. Four o'clock. By five, her brains were boiled up into a frenzy of anger and jealousy, so that when Shay's key eventually clicked in the lock, she was ready to explode.

"You bollocks!" she yelled "Where were you?"

"Working," said Shay, with utter nonchalance, although his own brain was fairly boiled up too, largely due to the cocaine that the bar staff consumed to "keep their energy up."

"How dare you stay out all night and leave me sitting here like an old granny?"

"You're not a granny," spat Shay. "You're just a frightened little girl."

She left Boston on a Greyhound bus the next day, with a ten-day ticket to anywhere. She stayed on the bus for days, sleeping fitfully against the rough upholstery or staring out at the sheer expanse of America. From her dusty window seat, one little long-distance bus on the freeway seemed like the biggest place on the planet to be alone. But she wasn't frightened—she would do this trip herself.

Out West, far into the desert, she stopped to stay in a motel because it had a gigantic polar bear in the lobby. Poor creature, she thought, a polar bear in the desert. About as big a freak as she was here.

To be on the safe side, she'd been sending her dollars home from Boston each week to put toward her college fees. By the time she found herself in West Texas, she'd spent more money than she'd meant to, and she was running out of cash.

That was when she came across Benny's. Lori the waitress said they were looking for staff, and she could use a roommate. So she joined the groovy Benny's Family Team and now—well—it was like one of those country-and-western songs, really: She was a waitress in Texas—on the run from a broken heart. Good job she had those flat shoes.

The first few weeks were okay. Texas was about as far from South County Dublin as you could get, culturally. Everything was oversized, from food portions to pickup trucks. The rich were garish and the poor were brown. The heat was astonishing: She would emerge from the air-conditioned diner in the middle of the afternoon after the morning shift and feel like she had been thrown into a sauna. In the bars, the men had real cowboy hats and real guns, and even though they were speaking English, she could barely understand what they were saying half the time.

On her nights off when she and Lori headed into town, she loved driving down the freeway—like a concrete river flowing briskly across the prairie. However, more and more of late she was getting these odd, searing pangs of desire for the sea of all things; it was like a strange kind of claustrophobia. It had really begun to upset her that she was miles away from open waves. Her primal drive as a briny beast was coming out at last. *Landlocked* was what sailors called it.

"Table nine, *por favor!*" Ai Liên yelled into the kitchen.

"*¡Sí, Chinita!*" answered Anselmo, grinning. "When I teach you Spanish?" Anselmo had a crush on Ai Liên.

"Hey, I'll make your dinner salads," said Kate, laughing. "You bring out the main course." Ai Liên was balancing two plates on her right forearm and two others in each hand, flawlessly. She was blessed with a feline sureness, never getting flustered and never complaining; always solidly in control. She worked only a couple of night shifts each week, to supplement her husband's income, presumably. Kate liked to imagine how some sweet soldier boy had sent for her, after getting back from his final tour of duty, or spirited her onto one of the last choppers out of Saigon. Now the neat clapboard house, the man, a kid . . . and a dog in a station wagon maybe. Kate needed to mold the sketchy facts into bad cliché only because it scared her that she should so envy this girl's easy assurance, her security.

She followed Ai Liên out with three more plates as the diners marveled over the food. Chill, dudes, she thought, this is only Benny's. But she just smiled. Ai Liên smiled too. Back at the salads station, as they dolloped spoonfuls of orange and white gunk over bowls of pale lettuce, Ai Liên stuck her face into Kate's and smiled again, crossing her eyes and bucking her teeth, and they laughed.

She could only have been about twenty-two, Ai Liên, but sometimes she seemed the oldest person in the restaurant, so silent and, according to the other staff, cold. But Kate admired Ai Liên's crafted reserve. No petty backbiting like the others, and always gracious. Her capacity for work was amazing and on top of that she was beautiful. No one could fault her, and no one could hurt her either. Kate bet no jerk had ever cheated on Ai Liên.

In the beginning they barely spoke, but it was hard not to get to know people on the graveyard shift. After one o'clock or so, there was a lifeless stretch until about five or five-thirty in the morning, when the truckers and early shift workers flooded in. Then there would hardly be time to breathe until the day shift arrived at seven-thirty.

Ai Liên didn't ask questions, so neither did Kate. They talked, instead, of Europe, of California, or of movies, and in the quietest hours, attempted conversations in French.

"My kid's birthday yesterday," Ai Liên said, suddenly sidling up to Kate behind the counter. The place was dead. "I got photos next day."

Kate was honored as Ai Liên handed over the envelope of pictures she'd been looking at earlier. The first photo showed a very handsome little boy, sparkling at the camera, beside a cake that read HAPPY 8TH B'DAY JIM in blue icing. Kate did a double take. Surely Ai Liên wasn't old enough to have a kid that big?

"He's really beautiful," Kate said. Ai Liên gleamed, and the child echoed out of her eyes briefly. There were a few snaps taken around what looked like a very small and surprisingly sparse apartment, some fuzzy ones of Ai Liên in a kitchen, the little boy at school, and one of an old woman holding her hand up to the lens to shield her face, laughing.

"Is this your granny? Are the rest of your family here too?"

"This my family," Ai Liên said. "Other family . . . gone now. This my grandmother's sister. She takes care of my kid, I take care of her."

"And where's your husband?" Kate found herself blushing as she realized too late that she shouldn't have said it. Ai Liên's facial muscles barely flinched.

"My kid is very good boy. He very clever in school. We are very happy now." She was hesitant, flicking through a few more photos before she spoke again. "I leave his father . . . three years ago."

"Me too!" Kate spluttered. "I mean, I left!"

She fished her bag out from under the counter clumsily. She had only one photo of Shay, the one she kept only so she could throw it out one of these days, except that she never did. Ai Liên looked at the blurry snap taken the previous Christmas.

"You still carry him around?"

Kate's face dropped at Ai Liên's sharpness. She missed Shay, despite it all. She continued looking through the photos, mostly of the child, the old woman, and one of a smiling Ai Liên in brown polyester, wearing a stars-and-stripes party hat. Ai Liên pointed at that one.

"See—me as a nice Asian American chick!" She chuckled with a tumble of unexpected laughter and disappeared in the direction of her table.

In the last snap of the pile, the tiny, wizened old lady sat engulfed by a massive armchair with tattered covers. In this shot she frowned over the birthday cake directly into the camera. She wore Western clothes, oversized and ugly, and her eyes, hidden deep within an armor of leathery, creviced skin, were mistrustful and angry, her mouth fixed in a tough but weary line.

Kate's knowledge of Vietnam was limited to the standard images: the little girl running along the road toward the camera, her clothes burned off by napalm, the Saigon army captain shooting a man in the head. Shell-shocked blond boys with blank faces. But as she looked at the grandmother's face, she realized the most disturbing thing was the covert horror behind the eyes, concealing experiences that Kate could not even begin to imagine.

It was three o'clock now, and very quiet. She pulled the tattered photo out of her uniform pocket and there was Shay grinning, with a pint in his hand and a glittering tree behind him. He had that stupid, endearing look on his face that used to induce a Kate all-systems shutdown.

Ai Liên interrupted her dreaming, motioning over to the window.

"I don't bloody believe it," said Kate. "This bunch look like trouble."

They watched in dismay as a stream of college boys in sweatpants poured from a huge bus and into the restaurant. They were loud, mostly drunk, and they crowded into the entire side section of the place, which was usually cordoned off this late at night. They all wanted to order at the same time.

Kate was frayed and her head was splitting. As she wrote down their orders, the words jumped around the notepad like stoned spiders. Ai Liên glided around smiling, noting, placing dishes. They took care of the rest of the tables quickly and by then it was time to pick up the bus party's main courses.

"How can you stand these creeps?" Kate snapped.

"These guys are pussycats," said Ai Liên. Kate stared back, making a face. Ai Liên shrugged, "No guns . . ."

Soon there was a pileup at the hatch, of course. Thirty tables were running full blast, and they'd no busboys or backup; the orders were getting confused. Table seven was calling for the manager.

Kate was forgetting the hash browns and the french

fries. It was a long time since she'd felt this angry about anything besides Shay. She and Ai Liên were literally running around the restaurant, Manolo the cook was shaking as he rushed to prepare the food, and the situation suddenly struck her as intolerable.

"Let's walk out," she said. "Let's just walk. . . . Don't you see what's happening here? They have no right to assign only *two* waitresses for the entire night shift. They pay us less than the minimum wage, no health insurance, and then have the nerve to understaff us. When it's this busy we don't get tips anyway!"

Ai Liên said nothing and carried out two burgers, which enraged Kate even more. She grabbed Ai Liên's arm on the way back into the hatch.

"Maybe you're just really happy to be part of the Benny's Family Team, is that it? They're working your butt off and you're just taking it. Let's leave, I'm telling you. We'll all just go, walk out."

Ai Liên turned on her furiously. "We are only two waitress here tonight. You want to leave me here, alone? You leave me, by myself?"

Anselmo had joined Manolo at the hatch now, watching this outburst from the usually silent Chinita with some awe.

"With them, now four workers—for whole place. So we help each other—we all work same. That what means fight. We all work—that is fight. Also, shut up, because you nice white girl, speak English. You do what you like. I need this job. Manolo, Anselmo need. If you work here, this is what you get. Just fight. You say *screw you, screw you, screw you*—inside. Outside—you *smiling!*"

Ai Liên smiled again: charmingly, calmly, and walked back out to the restaurant with her usual feline step. Kate stood there openmouthed.

Manolo started to chuckle. "Now you know how *los Vietnamitos* won the war, *Mamí.* . . ."

Kate cleaned up the student mess after that, and Ai Liên tended the remaining tables. When she went back into the main section a while later, the fans hummed, the coffee machine steamed gently, and the fray was no more. Ai Liên was leaning against the register near the entrance, gazing out the window. Kate approached quietly.

"I'm sorry, Ai Liên. I shouldn't have lost my head."

"Is okay."

"You know, I wouldn't really have left you."

"Why not you leave? Why are you here? You free— no kid, no man. You can do anything."

Kate, for the second time that night, was speechless.

"Why you here?"

"Why? Because I got off the Greyhound and saw the 'help wanted' sign."

"So maybe also now you get back on Greyhound."

By six o'clock the tables were filling up again. They had the usual truckers and early travelers. The freeway outside kept catching her eye with its cargo of cars and trucks as they tore past in garbled lines, silenced by the double glazing. It wasn't really a freeway, then, since you could only go in one straight direction. And it was a thousand miles down it to the sea.

She got a brief, hallucinatory whiff of ocean air— Dollymount strand's wooden bridge creaking under a steady stream of cars, the beach vibrating with the heat. There was a certain sweet loneliness about losing sight of land on the ocean, but to lose the scent of the sea was terrifying. She wondered how long it would take to get to a coast.

She almost didn't notice Ai Liên coming up behind her around six o'clock, her face flushed cherry red and hands trembling.

"Please, Catri-*nah,* do me a favor." She was the only one who called Kate by her real name, putting a funny emphasis on the last syllable. Her voice was even quieter than usual.

"Of course, what is it?"

"Swap tables—please?"

Kate walked, slightly mystified, to the other end of the restaurant, with the coffeepot in one hand and menus in the other. The number fourteen window booth was jammed with three large men, one sporting a Stetson, another in military garb, and a third in civvies with a crew cut. From ten feet away, they looked like trouble; either military or ex-military, probably from the base due south of Roxton.

"Hah, honey. First, we'll have three coffees and some ice water, and some O.J."

"And get me some cigarettes from the machine, sweetie." The fat one who was filling the place with smoke pushed two dollars toward her with flabby, suet-colored fingers. He was in his early sixties, in a white shirt that strained against his belly. She placed the menus on the table and turned away to get the coffees.

When she returned, she noticed that there was one other customer at the table. Scrunched in between Laurel and Hardy was a tiny Asian girl who came up to the level of the fat man's elbow. A wave of horror prickled over the back of Kate's neck. The girl was about thirteen, and she stared up at Kate with huge, empty eyes before turning her face into the man's upper arm like a child. She made no sound.

"Sorry, I'll get another menu," she began.

"Don't worry, sweetheart," said the skinny guy. "She don't read none!"

After Kate took their order, she turned to the girl.

"What would you like, miss?" No response, just the dark eyes, transmitting nothing.

"Oh, yeah," said the big man. "Well, I guess mah wife will have a large chocolate milk shake then. Won't you angel, *a milk shake,* huh, *milk shake?*"

She nodded and turned her head in toward his arm again. Kate wrote it down. One large chocolate milk shake. For his wife.

Ai Liên avoided Kate for the next hour until table fourteen were well gone and they both found themselves waiting at the hatch. She smiled in a strange, icy way.

"Now you see the guys not pussycats."

"They were the ones with the guns?"

"Guns, bombs, mines, tanks—everything!" Ai Liên laughed briefly, although what she said was clearly not meant to be funny.

"That girl was Vietnamese?" Ai Liên nodded.

"How old?"

"Depend how much money this guy have. Younger, more expensive. When I got to the refugee camp, already I was seventeen. Not so expensive."

For one second, as Kate looked into Ai Liên's face, it was the face of the old lady in the last photograph. Ai Liên's features seemed to camouflage a similar, covert horror. Almost unconsciously, she touched Ai Liên's arm, but Ai Liên flinched away with a flicker of pure anger.

When Mr. Daly and the other staff arrived in at seven o'clock, Kate left the busload-of-students crisis unmentioned. She quit instead.

"But you only been here a month," began Mr. Daly.

"I have a new job on the coast," she lied. "By the way, I need to speak to Ai Liên before I leave."

"She's gone already, on account of that day job of hers," Mr. Daly said as he calculated the night's accounts. "Shore beats me how that little bitty girl can do double shifts midweek."

"Day job?"

"Yup. Texas Instruments. Guess she needs the extra money, after that no-good husband dumped her."

Kate felt light, as if somebody had just pulled open the curtains in a sickroom. She began to realize what Ai Liên's few words of advice to her had meant. *You can do anything. . . .*

There was no reason for Kate to be out here, in the middle of nowhere, landlocked. There was no reason for her to hide, or sit waiting in the dark for anybody—ever. Outside, the freeway was glittering with vehicles in the early-morning sun. *So maybe now you get back on the Greyhound bus.*

In the toilet, Kate threw the flat shoes into the stainless steel garbage can and pulled on her boots. She removed Shay's picture from her pocket without looking at it. Holding it over the grubby yellow porcelain sink, she took her lighter with *Benny's—A Home Away from Home* in gold print on the side, and lit one corner of the picture. It began to curl up, emitting multihued and malodorous smoke.

As the flame reached her fingers, she dropped it into the sink and watched it disintegrate, into brown and black powdery ashes. Then she ran the faucet and sluiced it away down the drain. She realized now that Shay wasn't so completely bad, he just didn't want the same things she did. And if she wanted different things, then she was the fool to be waiting around for Shay. She was willing to bet that this fall, he wouldn't be back home in time for college.

College: the bustle in the morning corridors, the smell of new books and the excitement of a thousand new faces. This year she'd get to concentrate in her two favorite subjects, maybe even get to do a field project in Greece next summer. She could just picture Professor Breen's eccentric hand motions as he addressed the hall, she could hear the buzz of students fill the common room, cozy in the Dublin winter evenings. Or smell the Guinness and cigarettes in the crammed student club. Not to forget the ritual of coffee on the middle floor with Ciara. Ciara Donovan would be back soon from Germany where the others had gone to work, full of mad stories, no doubt. Well,

Kate had been all across America in a Greyhound bus and back; she'd have a few stories herself.

Outside, the BENNY'S FAMILY STEAKHOUSE sign had stopped revolving as she walked underneath it toward the back road that would take her to the Roxton bus. This afternoon, she would drop by the Greyhound depot for a ticket to the West Coast.

As she got to the corner, she heard a car horn behind her. Ai Liên waved as she was about to turn off toward the highway in the other direction in her old green Chevy. Silhouetted in the car's interior with the pristine sky of West Texas framing her face, she was again the nice Asian American girl Kate had imagined, a young mother in a big American sedan, without a man or a station wagon and no neat clapboard house. But she was . . . *smiling*.

Kate raised her hand in a goodbye wave, and found herself smiling back.

Helena Mulkerns

Helena Mulkerns was born in Ireland and has worked as a journalist, writer, and translator on both sides of the Atlantic. Her short fiction has been published in numerous anthologies and publications and has been nominated for the Hennessy Awards in Ireland and the Pushcart Prize in the United States. She currently lives in Guatemala. Contact her at her Web site, http://siar.net.

THICKER THAN WATER

by Emma Donoghue

So Mammy's getting married. Again, I mean. She was married to Da for twelve years before they got divorced, and then she had two boyfriends, Mark and Jimmy—one after the other, I mean, not at the same time—but we never thought she'd marry either of them. Donald's different, he's from England and older, like—eleven years older than Mam, which is a bit disgusting if you ask me. Not that anyone would. Mammy doesn't ask me or Ginny, she just says, "The wedding's the first weekend in June, girls, at the Belfast Royal Hotel."

That's four different men she's done it with, that I know of. There could be scads more of them, I suppose. It's hard to imagine. I'm still a virgin though I wouldn't shout that out at school. Sometimes I

wonder how I'll lose it. Melanie McGabbon lost hers
in the bit of grass behind the community center. I
don't think I'd fancy that. I'm going to wait till I feel
like it, I don't believe that rubbish about you have to
start before sixteen or you'll never be any good at it.
And I'm going to be picky about the fella too. These
days, you wouldn't know what you'd catch. It's con-
fusing, in fact, the whole business. When they're going on about how fabby it is, they make it sound like
Belgian chocolates, but then when you hear about
AIDS and stuff, it sounds like eating half a Mars Bar
you've picked up off the street.

Anyway. The wedding's going to be a big knees-up
even though Mammy claims she and Donald can't really afford it but after all, you don't get wed every day
of the week. Ginny pipes up and wants to know do the
two of us have to go or is it just for old folk. Mammy
asks does that include her, and Ginny gives her one of
those sulky wee smiles that always get round the
adults. So then Mammy says the two of us can invite a
friend each to make it less boring, how about that?
But Ginny gives this enormous shrug and says she
doesn't think any of her friends would want to come,
actually.

Which is typical Ginny. Half the time she's a messer
and half the time she's a selfish pig. She irritates the

skin off me. See, her name's really Virginia, after some old school friend of Mammy's, but since last Christmas she's been insisting we all call her Ginny, she won't answer to anything else. It's typical her, to change her name to something that sounds so like mine. I'm Jean—always have been—and now if there's a phone call for one of us, and Mammy shouts upstairs, you can't tell if she's saying Jean or Ginny. I bet she did it on purpose—like when she borrows my suede jacket and thinks I won't notice. Or when she leaves her Walkman turned on till the batteries wind down, then swaps them for mine, even though I keep telling her if she does it again I'll cut all her hair off in the middle of the night.

Also, my sister's got the attention span of a goldfish: two seconds max. Life's a perpetual shock to the lassie. She'll race around with her laces undone—trainers thumping—and then she's all astonished when she trips over a curb. And the worst of it is, it's usually me that has to bloody rescue her. The way I see it, it's none of my beeswax what Ginny gets up to, I'm not her minder. But Mammy puts on that guilt-tripping face and says, "Oh, Jean, you have to watch out for your wee sister, you know how she is. Blood's thicker than water and all that."

The thing is, the cow's twelve already—I'm

fourteen-and-a-half—and how long am I going to have to run round after her? Is it going to be like this till I pass my GCSEs and I can get the hell out of here?

Not that Ginny likes me watching out for her; she calls me a nag. She doesn't seem to realize that if it wasn't for me she'd probably have fallen under a bus by now. She's like some butterfly that just flaps around all day.

Anyway. If she doesn't want to bring anyone to the wedding, that means there's a spare invitation floating around. So I hare off right away and phone two of my friends, Eddi (her name's Edwina actually but she's mad about Eddi Reader, she's got all her albums) and Denise. They both say they'd love to, specially when I tell them there's going to be champagne.

Mammy's raging when she finds out what I've done. "But Mammy," I say, "it's only as many people as if Ginny and I each invited one. It's simple math."

She hates me being logical, because she's no head for logic herself. "Don't you simple-math me, girl," she says then. "Fifteen quid a head this wedding's costing me and Donald."

But I can tell it's not really about the money; Mammy thinks I've pulled a fast one. For a second I feel like giving her a wallop across the face and screaming, "Who wants to go to your stupid second wedding anyway?"

But I don't. That would be more Ginny's style.

It turns out the two of us are going to be brides-maids in pale pink, lashings of lace. Sexy, *not*. We're over at Mrs. Percy's for a fitting, and the woman starts tut-tutting over Ginny's chest, or lack of it. "Not a lot in the bosom department, have you, child?" says she with one of her wheezy laughs. Ginny's got this puss on her like she's been mortally wounded. It's true that her dress falls straight down from her neck whereas mine has a nice curve to it. When Mrs. Percy goes up-stairs to look for another spool of pink thread, I say, "Maybe you should wear falsies."

Not a peep out of my sister.

"You know," I say, "those rubber ones. You put them in your bra."

Now Ginny doesn't even need a bra yet. Mammy got her one last year because all her friends were wear-ing them, but Ginny forgets to wear it, and it makes no difference anyway. She scowls at me now and says, "I may have to go to this wedding but I don't have to wear fake tits."

"Only a suggestion," I say, sort of lofty. "Just trying to help you look more normal. Some hope!"

So Ginny starts tugging the dress over her head and rips the seam, wouldn't you know.

The morning of the wedding she goes out on her Rollerblades and doesn't come back for literally hours.

I'm raging. How can someone who dashes everywhere end up always being late? I don't know what the wee fanny does with her time but it all gets squandered.

When she finally clatters in without a word of sorry—like she's forgotten what day it is—I tell her, "We'd have gone without you, I swear to God."

She ignores that. She's busy climbing into her dress. She hasn't even had a wash as far as I can tell. I just wish we were wearing different colors so people mightn't realize we were sisters.

"What d'you think of Donald, then?" she asks, fairly quiet.

I give her a stare. Of all times to start asking. "He's fine," I say sharply. The fact is, it doesn't matter what we think of the man, it's too late now. It was too late the day Mammy told us the wedding was all arranged.

Ginny shrugs. She doesn't say anything else. I finish tying my sash in a bow and I steal a glance at hers, which is all lopsided but that's her business, if she wants to shame this family, let her. I can't find my tiny pink shoulder bag that I got for two quid in the Salvation Army shop; I'm looking everywhere.

"It clashes," says Ginny, dangling my bag by the strap.

"It does not," I tell her, holding out my hand for it.

"It's not the same pink."

"It's not meant to be, moron." All at once I'm nearly screaming. "It's a darker shade but it's the same family, Mrs. Percy said."

Ginny swings it up in the air and catches it like a ball. "What d'you need to lug a bag around today for anyway?"

I try and grab it from her but she pops it open and empties it onto the sofa. Mirror, lipstick, mascara, inhaler for if I get my asthma, spot concealer, one Polo mint in case of bad breath, one tampon in case of emergencies, two painkillers ditto. "My god," says Ginny, "you are such an anus!"

"I am not."

"Jean, if Jesus Christ knocked at the front door to take you up to heaven, you'd say 'Hang on, Jesus, I'll be needing my bag, and where's the key to my bike lock?' "

I roll my eyes and start fixing my mascara.

Ginny keeps poking through my stuff. She grabs the tablets. "Drugs! I'm telling Mammy."

"They're aspirin," I say coldly, prizing them out of her hand. I must be hurting the finger I'm bending back but the girl doesn't make a sound. There's nothing she'd like more than to have me accidentally break her finger; then she could run crying to Mammy, today of all days.

I drop the tablets back into my bag. "Stress can bring on periods, it's a well-known fact." I say this mostly to embarrass Ginny because she's only had about three and she hates them. She's still too mortified to ask for tampons in the newsagents, she goes all the way down to Boots so she can get them off the shelf.

"Stress!" she snorts.

"Well, it probably doesn't get much more stressful than going to your own mother's wedding."

"I thought you liked him? The Englishman?"

"Oh, Ginny, grow up." There's no time for this kind of carry-on. My little bag won't close now; I shove the tampon down the side. "Aren't you bringing anything yourself?" I ask, just to tease her.

She shakes her head, hair in her eyes. I did tell her to put gel in it.

"You'll probably start synchronizing with me, you're such a copycat," I say, fixing the silk rosebud behind my ear with a clip.

"I am not."

"Suit yourself. But you don't want to ruin the day by bleeding all over the altar, do you?"

"No," says Ginny, "what I don't want is to carry round some stupid little bag that clashes with my dress."

Now the door rings, and when I look out the window it's Denise and Eddi. "You just watch yourself today," I warn my sister. "I'm not having you make me look stupid in front of my friends."

She rolls her eyes, like she's about to fall into convulsions. "Oh, Jean, that'd be impossible," she drawls, "you're such an expert on everything."

I ignore that and run down to open the door. Eddi says my pink bag is just perfect, and Denise teases me about looking so buxom in my dress, which I don't really mind though I pretend I do. Nobody says anything much to Ginny, who's stomping round trying to remember where she put her pink satin wedding shoes.

"Oh my God," says Eddi, hanging out the window, "is that the groom?"

"That's him," I say, glancing down on Donald's hair, or what he's got left of it. I'm praying she won't say anything about how old he is.

"He's here!" Denise bawls down the corridor. "Mrs. Carter, the bridegroom's here!"

At this point I begin to regret having invited Denise, who was number two on my list as she's a bit excitable.

Mammy runs in now to see if we're ready. She's wearing Aunty Marie's cream wedding dress, which has a little red wine stain on the sweetheart neckline that Mammy's pinned a corsage on so you'd never know. "Mrs. Carter," squeals Denise, "you're not letting him in, are you? You're not letting him see you in your dress?"

"It's bad luck," says Ginny, muffled, from behind the sofa.

"Such nonsense," says Mammy, very snotty. "And, Ginny, what are you *doing* back there when the limo's waiting?"

"Can't find my shoes."

I knew she'd make us late. Didn't I say that's what she was like? So I stand there with Eddi and Denise, raising my eyes to heaven, while Mammy gets down on her knees in her wedding dress to scrabble round under the sofa. Then Mammy thinks to look in the wardrobe, and there's Ginny's shoes.

We get to the church bang on time. Apart from a baby down the back bawling its head off, and Donald developing a bit of a stammer, it all seems to go pretty well. I listen hard during the vows, wondering how I feel about my mother marrying someone who's not my father, but I don't seem to feel much of anything except embarrassed about wearing pink satin from top to toe.

After the dinner—I don't eat much because I'm

afraid of bulging at the waist—there's dancing. Mammy and Donald do a stiff sort of waltz, then the band plays seventies stuff and everyone relaxes. Me and my friends dance a bit and make comments about the guys, though there aren't many except for my totally uncool cousins and Donald's best friend's nineteen-year-old son, who's in the navy. Eddi and I get Denise to guess what "Voulez-Vous Couchez Avec Moi Ce Soir?" means, because she takes geography instead of French. Anytime I check, my sister's still slumped at the high table, picking at her slice of cake.

On my third glass of champagne I'm just starting to have a laugh. Me and Eddi and Denise are sitting at a side table with a good view of the navy guy, when I feel a tugging at my shoulder bag. I jerk round and there's Ginny. "What d'you think you're up to?" I whisper.

She scrapes her chair closer, mumbles something, and reaches for my bag again.

"What did you say?"

She clears her throat. "I think I've started."

"Started what?"

She's looking pale. "You know," she says miserably, staring at the little bag.

I get it then.

"What's the problem?" asks Eddi.

"The problem," I say, "is that Virginia here never thinks ahead. Isn't that the problem?"

"Ah, come on, Jean," says Ginny, looking at the floor.

I'm definitely enjoying myself now. "The problem is that she slags me for being so *anal* and then comes running to me for help. The problem is," I say in this very loud whisper, "that my wee sister's gone and got her period at the most awkward possible opportunity."

Denise falls about giggling and Eddi joins in.

Ginny tugs at my little bag. "Gimme. I need it."

The cheek of her! I pull the bag away. "Get one from the machine, why don't you."

"They never work," she says through her teeth.

"They do so."

"I don't have any change on me."

"You'll have to ask Aunty Maureen for money, then."

"I'm in a hurry!"

Denise laughs like a mynah bird.

I keep my fingers locked round my bag. "I told you this might happen. Why do you never listen? I've only got one tampon and I just might need it myself, ever think of that? You're so selfish!"

Ginny wraps her arms round herself as if she's in

pain, and squirms in the chair. "Please," she says, not looking at me. "I think I might be leaking."

So of course I let out this big dramatic sigh and open my bag. I mean, I was only messing before; I was always intending to give it to her in the end. I'm about to slip it to her discreetly under the tablecloth, but at the last minute I just can't resist. "Is this what you're looking for?" I belt out loudly, holding up the tampon so it's nearly in her face.

Just then the music happens to be at a quiet bit, so my words come out like a public announcement. Heads turn; even the navy guy stares over at Ginny, who's gone the color of an eggplant.

And then she does something peculiar. She doesn't even take the tampon, after all that, she just scrapes her chair back and stomps off across the ballroom.

She's only gone a few steps when I see the stain. Dark, shiny red on the back of her pink dress, as big as a baby's face. Everyone sees it. Mammy and Donald stop dancing.

Ginny looks at their faces. Her hand goes back; she feels the wet. She walks faster.

"Look at her!" says Eddi in my ear.

I launch myself out of my chair, tripping on my hem. I catch up with Ginny before she's halfway across the ballroom. She's going the wrong way; the loos are down the back corridor. "C'mon," I whisper, big-sisterly, "let's get you mopped up."

She shoves me out of her path and strides on. She's left a bloody fingerprint on my sleeve.

But that's not the worst of it. That's not the thing I can't get out of my mind, afterward, no matter how often Denise says it wasn't my fault and Eddi says these things happen.

What I don't think I'll ever forget about my mother's wedding day is the look in Ginny's eyes as she pushes me away from her: icy, astounded. As if I'm a stranger who's knifed her in a crowd. As if she's never seen me before in her life, and never will again.

EMMA DONOGHUE

BORN IN DUBLIN in 1969, Emma Donoghue is an Irish writer of stories, novels, history, and plays for stage and radio. Her books of fiction include *Stir-fry* (1994), *Hood* (1995), and a sequence of fairy tales for young adults, *Kissing the Witch* (1997). She lives in Canada.

OFF YA GO, SO

by Chris Lynch

I don't understand.

What's with all the music everywhere? Does everyone, I mean *every*one, think he can sing in this country? Everyone thinks he can sing in this country. Why do they do it? Why would they want to?

It rains every day here. Not like, a little rain. Not like, most days. It rains buckets and bloody buckets every bloody day.

Postcards. Traffic jam, Ireland. Blackface sheep standing in the middle of a road that wouldn't get you anyplace fast even if it wasn't blocked with blackface sheep. Sunsets gold and orange over Inis Mor or the Burren across Galway Bay. Great, but doesn't the sun have to come up before it can set?

Guinness. You are more likely to locate a shorty

leprechaun with a pot of gold than you are to locate a travel guide without a picture of some old geezer sitting in front of or under a pint of motor oil. Here they call it stout. "Creamy rich warming" is what they will have you believe, but if you are looking for what the rest of the world thinks of as beer and decide to do the local economy a favor by buying one of these mothers, which, by the way, take about as long to pour as it takes the average Irishman to whip off his version of the song "Carrickfergus," then you are going to receive a quick first lesson in Irish language: "Creamy rich warming" means, in English, flat soapy burnt.

And while we're at it. How do you say nine o'clock sharp, in Irish? Eleven-thirty. Doesn't anybody have anyplace to get to?

"Where you been? I been standing here forever, and those jugglers and mimes won't quit juggling and miming. This is the arts festival, right? Like, the world famous—"

"I've something to tell you, O'Brien."

She had never been serious before this. I mean, never. As relentless as the miserable weather had been through that entire alleged summer, that is how persistent Cait's cheeriness was. And it wasn't like that crap Celt sweetness from the Irish Spring commercials that make you want to puke and change your name from O'Brien to Stanislaus and never, ever use the soap or any other green products ever again. But this was real, she was real. I know, because I tested it every chance I got because, to be honest, I couldn't believe it. Couldn't see why a person should be so sunny in a place where the sun refused to shine.

She was like those palm trees and tropical plants popping up all over the West of Ireland. What's a nice flower like you doing on a rock like this? She stood out, Cait did. Maybe that was the thing. Maybe that was the why of it. Why maybe I did some things that possibly I shouldn't ought to have been doing.

So anyway, I took notice, when she got serious.

"Okay," I said slowly. "You have something to tell me."

I was supposed to be getting away from my "element" for the summer. Escaping Boston to encounter better things, you know, on the Emerald Isle. As if maybe it was sunlight that had been turning me to the dark side of the force. Ireland's basic goodness was supposed to right me. No place is *that* good.

Cait was, is, near as I can figure, my second cousin.

Something like that. I never was any good at the math. For sure, she is a relative of a relative. I know that because I met her at a clannish gathering of about a hundred people at what I guess was a farm even though it didn't appear to be growing anything much besides little stone buildings with no roofs. My arrival in Galway was an excuse for these folks to get together and have what they call a hooley. And holy hooley they did. I don't believe any one of them even noticed when I left after a couple of hours with Cait as my guide to the fun side. And for sure, Galway had a fun side.

The festival was a new thing then. Galway was a new thing. Fastest-growing city in Europe, was the word all over the radio, all over the *Galway Advertiser*. For the first few days that was a trip, fun, electric. Even when the caller to the Gerry Ryan show pointed out that Calcutta was generally considered to be the fastest-growing city in the *world*, but did that make it a good thing? I didn't care. What did I know about Calcutta?

It was all fine with me, since I was with Cait and Cait was choice in every way. We waded through the jugglers and the clowns and the big German tourists on the tiny little sidewalks of Shop Street and Market Street and the street that crossed them, Cross Street, and if I did get the temptation to make fun of the creative effort that went into naming the streets, and if I did act on that impulse, it didn't matter because Cait could smile through whatever I did. I think she liked to hear somebody takin' the mick out of the place.

Takin' the mick. Is that a phrase, or is that a phrase? Never heard nothin' like that before. I was taking that one home with me.

And I never held a girl's hand before. No kidding, I never ever did. I laughed for real the first ten twenty thirty minutes of it because it was just so nuts. I looked at Cait's little china-white hand inside my kind of gray-beige one, and I was just made to laugh, as she led me through the streets. She looked back, laughed at it too, but didn't let go.

Did plenty of other things with girls and hands before that. Never did the holding before. Lovely. That's a word too, isn't it? Lovely. They use it a lot. I knew of the word, but had never had occasion to use it, not one time in my life, before Galway and the arts festival and Cait. Go figure.

"You are lovely, you know?" I blurted out and blurted out that very first evening.

"Where ya goin' with that?" she asked. Amused. Surprised. But not really. "Enough of that carry-on, O'Brien."

We passed either the same spot, or a spot that looked a helluva lot like other spots, for the fifth time before I snapped a picture of a fiddler in front of a sweater shop. There are loads of fiddlers and sweater shops, but this guy had a beard like a full sheep was clamped on to his chin. So I snapped his picture with my disposable panoramic camera.

With his foot, he started pawing hard at his cap on the ground. Like a fiddle-playing trick donkey.

"He wants money," Cait said.

"Who doesn't? For what? For taking his picture?"

She shrugged.

I had never heard of such a thing in my life. Back home me and my boys would have resined his bow for him if he wanted to play that crap with us.

We crossed to his side of the street. I pulled a gigantic deer's head coin out of my pocket and tossed it in.

That was how it started. First night. First fine night of many fine nights.

"What made you pick Ath*lone*? Where is Athlone? And why?"

"Where," she said calmly, "is no place. Athlone is a town that isn't. Why, is because I'm related to about a million people around here, and so are you, I might point out. If I'm seen going into the local place I make all manner of trouble for meself."

"Oh," I said. "Right. Right, of course."

"I hitched. Not that you're asking."

"I'm asking, of course I'm asking, if you give me a chance."

We were sitting in one of the many dark cavelike coffee spots of the city at ten A.M. midweek. Not a great buzz in the city at that hour. Which was fine with us.

Cait slid a small pamphlet across the rough wooden table at me. I took it without looking.

"Have a scone, will you?" I said.

She shook her head. "I couldn't. Couldn't eat a thing. Sick."

"Right," I said, and picked up the pamphlet. I heard the flint of her lighter spark, followed by the deep intake of smoky breath. At night in this same place there is no need to light a cigarette to accomplish the same thing.

"I don't have any money," she said.

I looked up. She was smoking hard and fast now, in a way I had never seen her, or anybody, smoke. She was blowing out old smoke as hard as she could, sticking the butt back in her mouth as fast as she could to get the lungs refilled with new smoke.

"Please smile," I said. "Or at least unfrown. It's unnatural, and scary, to see you all puckered up like that. Please . . ."

"And I have no access to any money," she said.

The grim atmosphere, the smoke, the darkness, combined to give this the feel of some World War II spy scene, rather than the pointless nonstop fun we had been enjoying for weeks now.

"Okay, so don't worry about the money, Cait. I wouldn't ask you for the money. How much can these things cost anyway? It can't be—"

She came at me like an accountant. An angry accountant. "In addition to *these things*," she spat, "there is the ferry, or plane fare, the overnight in the—"

"Excuse?"

She sighed, a large dramatic smoke-dense angry sigh. "England," she said.

"England," I repeated, afraid to do anything more.

"England, O'Brien, is where one has to go."

"England. England? Why? Why not here?"

" 'Tisn't done here."

"Dublin. Dublin then, right? We can go there."

" 'Tisn't *done,* as in against the bleedin' law, right?" she said, somehow both more intensely and more quietly. "In fact, they're not even technically allowed to give ya *that*." She pointed her quarter-inch stub of a cigarette at the pamphlet, which I now realized gave all the important wheres and hows. In England.

"Christ," I said to the booklet, as if Cait were not still there. "I don't want to go to England."

She smacked her hand down on top of the booklet hard enough to make me jump. "Nobody bloody *wants* to go to England, do they now?"

I looked up, ready for the fight, but she was already done. Done with me, anyway. She was fumbling around in her raggedy bag, looking for the lighter again, shaking, cigarette clinging to her lips, tears emptying into her bag while she cried, cried, cried, cried.

I slid my hand flat across the splintery table, reaching for her, for her to take it. She slapped it. I left it there. She found the lighter, looked up at me. I wasn't going anywhere. She slapped my hand harder.

Before, though. When it was love. Before it got serious.

Westport, County Mayo. Westport House, this great old Georgian mansionlike thing surrounded by hills and gardens and its own pond with cute paddleboats, and inside, world-famous artworks and things you were definitely not supposed to touch but that were right there so of course somebody like me was going to touch them. I was always touching things I wasn't supposed to be touching.

"I'm just after tellin ya . . . ," Cait said when I had once again slid up behind her as she studied an oil painting of dogs about to shred a fox. I had my hands around her waist. She scolded me. I liked it. She did not move away, and she did not make me stop.

Down in the basement of wonderful Westport House, home of generations of folks with style and class and money and nice woodwork, they had installed a collection of stupid geegaws like the faucet that ran backward and a how-sexy-are-you machine, which probably would have made the previous owners puke. As we stood there, side by side, unable to step any farther into the place, Cait turned to me. "You'll be wantin' to take the mick out of this, I'm sure," she said.

Which would have been perfect, and right up my alley. Only I couldn't. I couldn't stop looking at her, and I couldn't think of anything to say.

This was my sweaters and poteen money. Poteen, the famous Irish hillbilly moonshine. It wasn't even my money. I was supposed to bring back sweaters and poteen for the boys. We even had a sweaters and poteen night arranged, first Saturday night after Labor Day. The boys were going to kick my butt when I got home with nothing. Unless I told them the story of how I got myself into this fix. Then they'd pat my back instead.

The boys were going to kick my butt when I got home.

My job was transportation and accommodation. Cait had already done the heavy sweating of making the clinic appointments. The pamphlet actually even had a section at the back with information on the most convenient and cheap places to stay in the area of the clinic, so that was what I was to work from.

"Right. And where did you hear about us then?"

I stammered, stumbled, leafed through the booklet which I had been so happy to close once I heard the man say that yes he did have vacancies.

When he couldn't wait any longer he worked it out himself. "You're calling from the Republic then, are ya?"

I nodded, sighed. He had heard this response before.

"Right, so what times are you scheduled for at the clinic, and when does your plane come in? We'll meet you. We'll take you around. We'll get you sorted."

Liverpool. Birthplace of the Beatles. That was what I knew about Liverpool. That was what everybody everywhere knew about Liverpool. Birthplace of the Beatles.

The man, Martin, picked us up at the airport like he said. Cait and I hadn't spoken during the bus trip from Galway to Dublin, nor the flight over, and we still weren't talking when Martin walked right up and picked us out of the small group disembarking.

"Mr. O'Brien?" he said.

I nodded.

He did a lot of quiet chattering in an accent I had to listen hard to if I wanted to get anything. Most of the time I didn't. He talked about the Beatles some. I knew plenty already about the Beatles.

I listened to Cait more. Listened to her breathing, since she wasn't speaking.

She looked out the window. Held my hand.

Martin stopped in front of what looked like a small version of the registry of motor vehicles back home. It was on a narrow street with a lot of other cold ugly stained square buildings.

"This is your hotel?" I said, trying not to sound too insulting.

Martin shook his head. "No time for that. This is the first clinic. I'll be waiting right here."

The first clinic, where Cait was to have her preliminary screening appointment. She pulled on the door handle and got out.

"Go on now," Martin said, shooing me along after her.

First we sat in a waiting room until a lady called Cait. I sat. Ten minutes later, we were reunited but directed upstairs to another waiting room. There we encountered five other girls, ranging between the ages of fifteen and forty or so. Two of them had guys with them. Nobody was talking. The light in the room was kind of shockingly bright, compared with the waiting room downstairs, and the street outside, and Liverpool. Bright, like fluorescent light, but yellowed, not white. We sat rigidly in our molded plastic chairs, flipping through *Hello!* magazine, which they had by the hundreds.

"She's Irish," Cait whispered, motioning toward a very young girl in a blowsy yellow dress. "And she's Irish," to the older lady in the two-piece tweed. "And so is she. That one . . . maybe."

Slowly, agonizingly, the staff made their way down the list. All the folks ahead of us disappeared into some exam room, to be replaced by newcomers.

They called Cait's name, and she jumped out of her chair as if she'd been cattle-prodded. I sat, reading about Pierce Brosnan and Sean Connery and Princess Diana when she was alive, and after.

Cait came out. Sat. They called her again, and this time she pulled me by the hand into the room.

"You will be paying, then," said a woman behind a desk, who looked too busy to be dealing with me.

"Ya, ya," I said. I started spilling notes all over the desk, the floor, the desk, looking at the woman, at Cait, at the floor, over my shoulder, like I was making a drug deal.

She gave Cait a card. "Be on time," she said.

Martin was outside, just like Martin had said he would be.

"You'll want to rest then?" he asked.

"Yes," Cait said curtly.

Martin's wife, Jane, led us up narrow corridors and stairwells, all well lighted and revealing busy sad wallpaper of horses and carriages and dogs and birds. On the third floor we were led into tiny room twelve. "If you be needin' anything . . . ," Jane said. She nodded. I nodded.

"Cheers," Cait said, which sounded very strange to me.

We spread ourselves out on the oversoft bed and tried to watch the TV, which was bolted onto a steel arm so close to the ceiling it was like watching a light fixture. It didn't matter. We could hear, so seeing it wasn't all that important. We had three hours before we needed to be back out again. Staring. Staring was what we were going to do.

"I've got to sit my exams this year," Cait said, panicky, at one point. "I don't know how I'm going to get through it, O'Brien. I don't know if I'll get through it."

"Well . . . you know, where I go to school we have exams every year. I try not to worry about it too—"

"Some of those girls are here by themselves. D'ya realize . . . they came all the way here, with nobody . . ."

She closed her eyes tight.

It was as much like a factory as anything. We ran into most of the same people from the other clinic. As if we all had been prepped, we did this little ritual thing. Make eye contact, nod slightly, look away. End of it.

Second floor. A nurselike person led us into a clean but ancient-looking concrete room with yellow painted walls. I sat while Cait got into a gown and into bed. I put her things into her bag, took out the Walkman, handed it to her. She placed it in her lap and stared straight ahead.

"Wish I had a cigarette," she said.

"I'll run out and get you some," I said.

"Hello," the boss-nurse-doctor lady said. She was all business. Not mean, not warm. "We all set then?" She was leaning over the bed, looking into Cait's eyes like a hypnotist. A woman, a girl, anyway, started crying loudly in the next room.

Cait didn't answer right away. This seemed like a place where they needed answers right away.

"All set then?" the woman asked more directly.

Cait's eyes went all blue water. "Don't know. Don't . . ." Cait looked at me.

Me. Right. Like I was . . . what? I could help, though. I could help, could be of help. I would help her now.

Cait kept looking at me. She had never once asked what I thought before now.

I'd never asked myself, as far as that goes.

She stared at me. I stared at her. I thought I could help. I thought I could say something. I felt my own eyes going.

"Right you are, then," the woman said calmly, firmly placing her palm on Cait's forehead and guiding.

Cait gave way completely, her head falling back, her eyes fixing on the ceiling. She attached the Walkman's headphones to her ears and switched it on. She played it loud. I could hear the music as clearly as if I was wearing the phones.

"We'll be in for you in a moment, dear," the woman said. Then she turned to me. "You can be back at half past eight. She should be ready around then."

"Oh," I said, looking up at the clock. It was three-fifteen. "Oh. Okay." I looked to Cait, who was not looking back. "I'll just wait a few more—"

"Half eight, then," the woman said, gently taking my hand and giving a small tug.

I waved at Cait as I was led out. She glanced over, waved weakly, and looked back at the ceiling.

Liverpool is huge. Must be ten times the size of Galway. And frosty cold. Not cold the way New England can get cold in the winter, but a different and somehow scarier cold, where the wind, which blows at a thousand miles per hour, picks up moisture off the river and the ocean and *drives* the dampness into your bones and your joints.

The Mersey was something shocking. It was like a small ocean of its own, with the piers and stone embankments, with the far coast being almost obscured in the mist and rain.

Rain. Hard mean rain that came in thin bolts more

like fiber-optic lines than drops. The Mersey had
waves. It had a life. Walking along the long and mer-
ciless wide walkway that ran along the river, I had
moments of panic, where it was obvious to me that
the driving rain, the chopping wind, the slapping water, were pulling together to haul my stupid self in
and under and gone.

It is so big, Liverpool. Birthplace of the Beatles.

Stopped into a place called Harry Ramsden's, which
is supposed to be famous for fish and chips. Had a
hamburger. Tasted like fish.

Then back to the long walk along the river. Still felt
like it was going to get me, but still couldn't resist it.
Went to the iron rail and leaned over. Couldn't stop
looking at it, breathing it. Walked some more. In the
middle of a sort of expanse of paved wind-beaten
nowhere, was a small Beatles tribute. Their signatures,
Paul and George and Ringo and John. In the ground.
From when they refurbished the area. Kind of a highlight. I reached down, and I touched them. Touched
George Harrison's letters.

Found myself then on hands and knees, running fingers over letters of names. Then looking at the whole
deal, the nearby bench. The walk, completely empty
of people. The river, raging and huge and ignored.

These were the Beatles, for God's sake. How is it

possible to make the Beatles, the *Beatles*, be here, all alone? Tiny and alone and sad.

Where exactly was she now? Which cold room? With whom? What were they doing with her exactly right now? What position had they bent her into? Was she awake? How many people were working on her? What were her eyes fixed on? Did it hurt? Was it over? Was it started?

She had never been to Liverpool before. Said she had relatives, which I guess meant I did too. Loads of Irish in Liverpool.

Walking and walking and walking and walking and walking. The streets are huge in Liverpool. Big and wide and slick with wet. The rain had quit but it certainly felt temporary. Nice buildings, even the ugly ones. Chunky, large, up to something. Monstrous ugly cathedrals. All of it quiet. Aside from cars, there appeared to be almost nothing going on whatsoever.

Albert Dock. There was stuff like this back home, loads of it, in fact. Old working-waterfront stuff that had been converted to shops and things. There were museums. I didn't go in. There were pubs and restaurants I stayed out of too. I walked around the Albert Dock, and around. Plenty to do there. Plenty of shiny, warm, and inviting inside space to spend an interesting few hours.

I looked in the door of the Maritime Museum. Liverpool, where all those Irish and the grubbier Irishlike English folks piled into boats to come to my country. Could have been the way my old man made the trip, as a matter of fact. Could have been. Could have been. Probably that would be an interesting thing to look into.

I closed the door of the Maritime Museum when the guy at the desk wouldn't stop staring at me. Went instead to the Beatles shop and bought a postcard of John Lennon in his round shades and sleeveless New York City T-shirt. Then I went back to walk along the Mersey.

"Yes, she is ready now. If you would like to go up to room . . ."

She was dressed, sitting up at about a sixty-degree angle with pillows piled behind her. Looking at a copy of *Hello!* magazine. She had the headphones on. I could hear them as I came up the stairs. From all I could tell she'd had them on like that the whole time. Do they allow that sort of thing? I hope they do. Hoped they did. I stood there in the doorway for a bit, watching her, waiting for her to look up. She looked okay, though not completely lifelike, suspended, like you can get when you have the headphones on and no-body else hears what you hear.

She looked up. There was nothing here or there on her face. She looked back down at her magazine, as if I was just another attendant passing by. Which is what all of them were doing, passing by, buzzing by, on their way to someplace else, on their way to somebody else. I got bumped three times in two minutes standing there. Busy place, this was. Too busy.

Finally Cait looked up again. This time, *at* me.

And then gone again. One hand flew up and covered her eyes, the tips of her fingers making obvious indentations into her temple. Tears escaped the grip anyway, falling down over her face and onto *Hello!* magazine until Cait's other hand came up and she held on tight, like to keep her face from blowing into fragments.

I went over and sat on the bed, collapsing into her. She grabbed me, she squeezed me, I squeezed her. I was drenched already, inside and out with Liverpool seep, but it hardly would have mattered. In my ear Cait was possibly trying to talk but what I was hearing was the persistent grasping of the air, as if I was hugging a racehorse or a steam train.

We left when they made us leave. It was the very last place on earth we ever wanted to be, but we could

not get ourselves up and out until we were made to.
When we got outside, Martin was there with the van.

We overslept.

"You're late," Jane said, knocking hard on the door.
Cait and I jumped. The television was still on, way up
there on the ceiling. I had no idea where I was. "You're
late," Jane said, knocking again. "You're going to miss
your plane."

"Oh God, no," Cait said desperately. She got half
out of bed, grabbed her abdomen, sat back.

"Go easy," I said. "Slow down."

"I can't stay here. O'Brien. I cannot stay here. I have
to go. I have to go home. I have to go home. I need to
be home."

"All right. Calm down."

"I have to go."

"Right, we'll get dressed and go."

"I have to have a bit of a shower. I can't—"

"Go. Go ahead."

I packed up while Cait showered. Jane came by again,
banging. "Ye'll miss your plane."

Cait was out of the shower. I looked at her. "You all
right?"

"Right, so," she said. "Off we go, so."

"Off we go, so," I said.

When we reached the bottom of the stairs, Martin was there finishing off a sandwich and jiggling car keys.

"Ye'll not have time for breakfast," Jane said, sticking two warm foil-wrapped packets into my hands. "But ye must eat. Here. Bacon and egg. Off ye go, so. G'wan now."

Cait reached over and held Jane's forearm, looking into her. She said nothing.

"*Slán,*" Jane said. "Off y'go, petal. You'll want to be gettin' home."

Cait squeezed, let go, and we hurried away.

The long bus journey between Dublin airport and Galway finally came to an end beside the Great Southern Hotel. The city was mad as it had been for weeks, buskers doing all the same tricks, bars spitting people into the streets, pipes and fiddles and guitars and *bodhran* and the odd digeridoo filling the air with noise, noise, arty party noise. We were back.

"My last two nights," I said, taking Cait's rucksack over my shoulder and her hand in my hand.

"I know," she said.

We crossed Eyre Square, where John F. Kennedy

once spoke, where Cait was approached by three different filthy girls who wanted to wrap her hair for three quid, and a guy with no teeth offered to sell me the tin whistle right out of his mouth for the price of a pint.

"Well, what I was thinking, was, I might maybe stay for a while. So."

Cait stopped, let go of my hand. Stepping up alongside of me as if she were unsaddling a horse, she removed her backpack from my shoulder. She kissed me, and at the same time grabbed a bunch of my hair.

"I think maybe not. So."

She walked ten yards to a bench, where a Gypsy-looking girl was set up with a hundred different colored threads and beads.

"Yes?" the girl said hopefully.

"Yes," Cait said. "That orange, that purple, and that metallic green."

"Beau-tee-ful," the girl said, and immediately set to wrapping Cait's hair.

I walked up and stood there, watching over the work for a bit. Cait rolled her eyes up to me. Reaching out, she grabbed my leg, just above the knee, and gave a small squeeze.

"Off ya go, so?" she said warmly. And for the first time since, smiled. Not the full-watt smile, but the spark of it anyway.

"Off I go, so," I said.

I waited for more. I expected more. Cait closed her eyes, listened as some girl standing on a box sang a wobbly version of something called "The Foggy Dew." Cait's lips moved along to the words. There was no more.

Off I went, so.

CHRIS LYNCH

CHRIS LYNCH is the author of many highly acclaimed books for young adults, including *Iceman, Shadow Boxer, Slot Machine, Extreme Elvin, Whitechurch,* and *Gold Dust.* He grew up in Boston and has lived in Ireland.

ABOUT THE EDITOR

GORDON SNELL is a poet, writer, and broadcaster who is the author of many books for young people. He lives in Dalkey on the coast south of Dublin.